A KISS FROM A REVENANT

KISS FROM A MONSTER SERIES
BOOK 6

CHARLOTTE SWAN

For those of us who want a love more powerful than death...

CONTENT WARNINGS

For a full list of content and trigger warnings please go to the author's website.
www.authorcharlotteswan.com

1

———

NORY

It's a mistake to be in the graveyard this late.

The Snowlands are dangerous in broad daylight. At night, there is a forbidding quality to the air. A sense that something dangerous lurks just out of view. Unease dances with the chill in the wind, entwining the two into one disconcerting mess. Despite it being mid-summer, the cold still lingers in the air, stinging my cheeks and nose as I look down at the familiar headstone.

It never changes, save for a few new cracks or a dusting of fresh frost. The sparse patch of grass cushions my knees as I wipe away the day's dirt from the plain inscription. *Mae Blynwood. Loved Eternally.* I've read it hundreds of times since it was first carved. I hadn't been sure what Mother would have wanted. The illness that claimed her life last year had come on suddenly and left little time for proper arrangements.

Lost in my own grief—and the seemingly endless amounts of work left in her wake—I had merely told the stone mason to do whatever was the cheapest. While my mother may have been the only seamstress in town, we were not a well-to-do family. After all the doctor's visits and the cost to bury her, the coins I had left could only afford the most basic inscription.

Still, I should've made sure to mention she was a mother. I have regrets about that.

Maybe that is why I come to visit every day. The guilt I feel over her passing has nagged at me. I have countless unanswered questions—lingering bits of conversation that will never come to pass. I wish to talk with her again, if only to ask for guidance and to absolve me of the guilt I feel for not being a better daughter.

My only solace is the steady stream of customers who need their clothing fixed. During the day, I can lose myself in monotonous work. The ghosts of my regrets remain trapped in shadow while I focus on the tasks at hand. Then the night comes, and the quiet stillness of the house is enough to make me go mad.

Moisture pricks at my eyes, and I hastily rub it away. Setting down the dreary-looking bouquet of roses, I touch the smooth stone. Without my mother here, I am truly alone—no husband to call my own. No father or extended family to welcome me in.

With all my current responsibilities, the idea of running my own household with a man of my choosing seems laughable. At twenty-four, many men in this town consider me well past the age of marrying. The ones that don't, well, I'd sooner marry a wild animal than bind myself to them in matrimony.

My pride and stubbornness have always been in lock step with each other. It has only been recently, and in the deepest parts of my grief, that I wish I had someone to turn to—who would shoulder some of this burden even if I did not love them. I would not be the first woman in this town to settle into an unsavory pairing out of necessity.

Life in the Snowlands is not an easy one. Our provincial town is nestled between two mountain ranges and at the mouth of a frozen shore. It is remote enough that anyone wanting to disappear can. In the winter, the sea freezes, and all incoming trade routes are completely blanketed by snow and ice. Meaning if someone were following you, they'd never brave a journey this far north and risk death.

That is why the Snowlands have become a haven for a rougher crowd.

Sell-swords, thieves, royal assassins—all manner of dangerous men call the Snowlands home. Once again, I kick myself for being out here this late. It would take nothing for a drunkard to happen upon me all alone.

However, a violent man is not the only thing to fear here.

Glancing up at the sprawling tree line, *The Woods* surround the graveyard. The massive evergreen and oak trees overlap like gnarled fingers. Inside, creatures scatter; the darkness beyond the first row of trees seems endless. My mother had told me stories of the monsters that call that infernal forest home. Along with her stories, there was always a stark warning to keep away from them, unless you were prepared to pay the ultimate price.

The memory of my mother comes rushing forward, overwhelming me with a sense of despair that makes me turn from the dark woods. I miss her, but more than that, I miss the companionship of another. When I was younger, I had dreams of leaving this town—seeing the world behind our frozen wasteland—but as I got older, I had made peace with the fact that my mother would need me. When we worked together, there was happiness, and I was content. At least, I was content enough not to complain or create idle fantasies of a life beyond my reach.

All that awaits me now is a vacant house and endless piles of mending to be done. Am I cursed? Is this truly all I have? To lead a solitary life without love, with no one to call my own. Am I doomed to the same fate that befell my mother, only without a child to take care of? Will I become a wraith who haunts the grave of my mother until I join her in the cold ground?

A bitter laugh escapes me.

"If it comes to that," I whisper into the cold night, "who would even know to bury me?"

One name comes to mind, and it sends a shiver down my spine. The only solstice is knowing that by the time death calls me home, he will have already come to his end. Before my mother's passing, I had the chance to marry, though I cannot say I would have been better off than I am now. Besides, I'd never agree to marry that horrible, deplorable, *vile*—

A twig snaps behind me, and I gasp. Whirling around, I see nothing, only the jagged shadows cast by the full moon above. A loan owl hoots in the distance. The night is still. That is, until my eyes snag on something unusual.

A loan figure appears at the edge of *The Woods*.

Tall, forbidding, and looming just out of sight. My heart races, pounding against my ribs, and then, as if I had imagined it, the figure is gone. In the blink of an eye, the treeline is empty, and a cold breeze caresses my cheek. Unease permeates inside me even as I sag with relief. Rising on shaking knees, I wipe the dirt from my dark skirt and turn from my mother's grave with the promise of visiting again tomorrow.

I barely make it a step before my blood ices over. I should not have come here tonight—I knew it was a mistake. My mother would've understood me missing one singular visit. For now, I am trapped here all alone as I stare at the one person I desperately avoid at all costs.

Lord Gunnar. He leans against a crumbling tombstone, arrogance dripping from every line of his posture. His arms are neatly folded over his enormous chest while his beady eyes roam over me. It had barely been a week since I last saw him. He had come to my house seeking repairs for the jacket he's currently wearing. One of the buttons had come loose, and I fixed it for him on the spot, not wanting to see him again to collect the item. With the steady stream of customers I had had that day, there had rarely been a moment that left the two of us alone.

The entire time, my hands shook, causing several pricks from the needle along my thumb. He had chastised my carelessness and used it as an opportunity to make more demands of me. The same demands he'd been making for almost ten years. He'd been vying for my hand since I was sixteen, and his first wife had died that spring in childbirth. The mourning period for his wife lasted as long as it took to bury her the next day. Since then, he has made his interest in me known despite my countless refusals.

I assumed that as I got older, his interest would fade to another poor girl. Yet, he has been as insistent as ever. He even accosted me at my mother's wake, telling me how it was not a lady's place to work and that I would soon follow her into the grave. If I were to marry him, my only responsibilities would be to bear and rear his children—a simpler life.

And one I would surely perish in just as his first wife did.

I refused him then, and I continue to deny him every few weeks when he reappears with another offer. Luckily, I've become very good at avoiding him, and blessedly, we've never been alone for more than a few minutes. Now it seems my luck has finally run out. The graveyard is remote, no one would know I was here unless—unless he followed me.

My stomach hollows at the thought even as I plaster a patient smile on my face.

"Lord Gunnar," I say, my voice carrying in the quiet night. "You gave me a fright."

He grins, moonlight glinting off his golden tooth. Taking long, slow strides over to me, my hands slip beneath my cloak, where I find the dull head of my simple dagger. The Snowlands have taught me better to be armed than sorry.

"You shouldn't be out here all alone, Nory," he chides. "Not with all those bodies going missing."

All the moisture leaves my mouth. I had heard whispers about these strange happenings from my customers. Only a few nights ago, the local morgue had been ransacked. We had a slew of graverobbers before, but they had only been after the treasures buried with the corpses. Not the bodies themselves. In this instance, the jewels remained; it was the bodies that were pilfered. It was not long before they reappeared at the edge of *The Woods*.

The corpses seemed to have been eaten by some animal: rotten flesh had been gnawed off, bones were broken or— in some cases missing—and strange puncture wounds had been along the necks and limbs of the bodies. Then came the live-stock, consumed in the same disgusting way and left to die in the open fields by whatever—or whoever—had found their way into our town.

All the more reason that coming out this late was beyond foolish.

"I was just heading home."

Giving Lord Gunnar a slight nod, I turn from him and begin the long journey back to my cottage. I don't make it very far when I feel a strong hand wrap around my upper arm. The scent of body odor and brandy overwhelms me as I'm pulled into Lord Gunnar's massive body.

"Nonsense," Gunnar purrs. "As lord of this town, it is my duty to see you back safely. Wouldn't want something to snatch you up."

His scent nearly makes me gag, but I manage to swallow it down. Giving him another fake smile, I gently try to dislodge from his grip.

"I appreciate the concern, sir, but really, I am fine."

Gunnar tightens his hold on me, drawing me closer towards

him. His dark eyes swirl with desire, and the gray streaks in his hair glow in the moonlight.

"Cease your struggling, woman. I insist."

"Lord Gunnar, please, let me go." His nails dig into my arm as I try to yank it away. The pricks of pain steal my breath. "You're hurting me!"

"Enough," he growls.

"Let me go!" I yell. "Stop this—I'll scream. Just let me go or—"

"Scream if you'd like." Gunnar's eyes darken as he licks his chapped lips. "No one will hear you. Even if they did, no one would stop me. This has been long overdue."

My stomach turns, and bile floods my mouth at the look he gives me. My struggling is futile, but I still thrash even if he does overpower me.

"What are you—stop!"

"If only you had agreed to be my wife," he sighs, "all this unpleasantness could've been avoided. I was planning on being gentle. Well, as gentle as a man like me can be. But now I see that you need to be brought to heel. Maybe then you'll remember your place."

I cease my struggling for just a moment. I need to stay smart and not panic. Giving in to fear will make this situation worse. Gunnar will give me an opening, and I have to be alert enough to take it.

Once he feels me go still, his grin widens, and his hand on my arm loosens by a fraction. His other hand comes up to skim over my shoulder. His rough fingertip traces up my neck and jaw.

"Now you see. Good."

His hand leaves my face to brush down my chest. Choking on bile, I stay frozen, holding on to my wits as best I can. My hand is still locked around the handle of my dagger. I wait and wait—until finally he does what I knew he would. Slip up. His other hand leaves my arm to work the strings at the front of my gown. That's my chance, and I take it.

With a swiftness I wasn't aware I possessed, the blade of my dagger whips through the darkness and slices clean across the lord's cheek. His scream echoes around us as he clutches at his face. Crimson blood pools from between his fingers as he stumbles back.

His dark eyes blaze with anger. I can't let fear freeze me. With haste, I gather the skirt of my dress and turn from the gruesome sight. His shock will only last so long, I must get away before—

"Bitch!" he screams. "You will pay for that."

I hear a click, and my whole body freezes. Dread courses through my veins as I slowly turn around. Still clutching his cheek, Lord Gunnar has produced a pistol in his other hand. It is perfectly aligned with my head. I could try and run, but he'd get a shot off before I got too far.

Hopelessness buckles my knees and nearly sends me to the ground. My life flashes before me. All of it was for nothing. I knew agreeing to be Gunnar's wife would kill me. Yet, it seems he's found a way of ending my life despite my best efforts. If I had left all those years ago like I had dreamed, this wouldn't have been my fate. Twenty-four years and I have nothing to show for it but a pair of scarred thumbs and a crumbling cottage.

Scenes from over the years play before my eyes in a pathetic montage. I am going to die before experiencing anything. Adventure, excitement, love—how am I to perish without knowing love? Without giving myself to a man and calling him my own? How—

There is a soft rustling sound, as if something is moving through the trees at a fast pace. Faster than any animal or human is capable of. I'm unable to turn my head, as Gunnar's finger is still tight on the trigger.

Maybe that's how I miss it—or I am already dead and this is all a hallucination because one moment I am staring at a loaded gun and the next Lord Gunnar is nowhere to be seen.

The spot he left behind in the grass is barren save for the two large footprints his boots disturbed. I let out a breath as my heart jams itself in my throat. Had I envisioned the whole thing? Was this some trick conjured up by my own mind as a manifestation of why it was unwise to come out here?

Slowly, I lift my hand and find the front of my gown. The laces of my dress are still untied, meaning...meaning it wasn't a delusion. Gunnar was here—he planned to do unspeakable things to me, and then he was gone. But how?

The graveyard is eerily quiet. The sounds of animals and rustling leaves are missing. There is only one low sound that cuts through the silence. It is out of place. It sounds wet— suctioning—the sound a mouth makes drinking the last dregs from a soup bowl.

Licking my dry lips, I survey the empty graveyard again. My heart pounds when I see them, nearly hidden by a fallen tombstone. There, amongst the broken stones, is a pair of polished hunting boots. Soft keening noises greet my ears as I approach.

I don't know why I'm heading that way—I should be running from this place while I still have a chance. Instead, I pad over, and what greets me is a gruesome sight.

Lord Gunnar is dead.

Or at least he will be very soon. His skin is pale, and his lips have turned blue. Those dark eyes that have looked at me with unbridled lust have turned milky and unseeing. His arms fall limply at his sides as one last wheezing gasp tumbles through his mouth. The only dead body I've seen was my mother's, and it was merely a glimpse before the doctor covered her in sheets.

I should be more transfixed by the sight, yet Lord Gunnar is not what my eyes land on. They are fixated on the bony hand holding his jaw and thrusting his face away. Pale skin stretches thin, highlighting each skinny bone and bumpy knuckle. I follow it until it disappears at the wrist under a dark cloak. The hood is up, and the head is buried at the juncture of Gunnar's neck and shoulder. Its body trembles, and the slurping sounds from its mouth reach me.

The sound makes my stomach roll as the creature pauses. Dropping his hand, Gunnar's body slumps over with a heavy thud and lies prone on the cold ground. My eyes return to the figure who stands, rising to its full impressive height.

Dull metallic clanks follow each of his stilted motions. A long, dark, tattered cloak slips down his back and drags along the dark grass. Before I can move, the creature whirls on me, and my whole world shifts.

The hood has fallen back, revealing a completely skeletal face. Hollowed cheeks and eyes are covered in the same waxy, pale skin as the hand. Inside the empty sockets, a fire roars; the light at the center is stark white. Rusty armor covers the rest of its body. The creature is massive—a foot taller than any man I have ever seen—and lean. Those blazing eyes stare at me, their color turning to a burning red with each passing second.

Blood covers his mouth and jaw. The scarlet liquid drips onto his cloak in a steady stream. Realization shocks me to my core. This is the creature that's been attacking the village. A creature my mother used to tell me stories of—how they lived between the world of the living and the dead. How they were infernal creations of dark magic that would devour you whole in the blink of an eye.

A demon, a monster—a revenant. An omen of death.

I watch in horror as its bony jaw unhinges and a pointed, dark purple tongue slips from between its sharp teeth. In one long salacious lick, it cleans the blood from its face. Its eyes burn as it stares at me, dipping towards my throat.

That breaks whatever strange spell I was under. With a bloodcurdling scream, I turn on booted feet from the horrors before me and run faster than I ever have from the graveyard—the gravel path I usually take echoes under my thunderous footsteps. More than once, I nearly lost my footing—slipping on uneven ground and my dress.

I pump my arms as my cloak and braid fly behind me. I don't dare slow down even as my legs and lungs begin to burn. I can feel his eyes on me—searing into my flesh even as I put distance between us. However, I don't dare look back, afraid I'll see him right on my heels. I speed up even as my body screams at me to stop.

It's not long until my cottage comes into sight. With one last yell, I power forward. Tearing open the front door, I slam it open and bolt it shut behind me. Throwing myself against it, I expect to hear the creature's footsteps pounding up the porch after me. Pressing my ear to the old wood, there is only silence save for my racing heart. My breathing is chaotic, and I'm left with no choice but to place my head between my knees and take some deep breaths.

Once I have calmed down enough to think straight, I slowly crawl to the front window and peer out. Nothing is amiss. The trees in the front yard blow in a gentle breeze. A bird lands on the railing of the porch before flying off on white wings. Everything is still and calm.

That doesn't stop me from bolting all the windows shut and sprinkling salt in front of them like my mother always did. I never thought I'd be so grateful for her superstitions. Once I am secure that the creature cannot gain entrance into my house, I let the evening play out in my mind.

I know what I saw. There is no denying that I crossed paths with a revenant tonight. He had been just as my mother described in her stories. Bloodthirsty—starving—wandering our world endlessly to satisfy itself. Pulling the curtains shut, I walk into the back bedroom and kick off my boots.

It makes no sense as to why the creature let me escape. I'm

not foolish enough to think I outran it. Had it wanted to capture me, it could've. Considering how quickly it took Gunnar, I have no doubt it could've snatched me up and drained me just as fast.

Yanking off my gown, I slide into bed in my simple shift and wool stockings. Exhaustion suddenly weighs me down. Regardless of the creature's motives, one good thing did come out of tonight. Gunnar is dead.

I no longer have to fear his demands or wandering hands. The constant need to look over my shoulder is gone. I feel a strange sense of peace. Even though it could not have possibly been his intention, the revenant had been the one to save me from Gunnar's torment. I am not foolish enough to think that he went after Gunnar for any other reason than that he smelled his blood and attacked.

Yet why had he not come for me? Surely leaving witnesses is unwise. I could've alerted the whole town to his whereabouts. So why didn't I?

I don't know, and even though it feels a bit silly, I say a silent thank you to the revenant. Intended or not, he did free me, and for that I am grateful.

Besides, it would've been very rude to repay my savior with an angry mob.

ERYX

y gaze remains transfixed on the splintered tavern door.

A white cloud puffs between my lips as I take another deep breath. There aren't very many people out tonight. No doubt word of my killings has spread, and villagers with common sense have chosen to remain safely at home. Still, some care more about their ale than their own safety. Or the foolish lot who thinks they could best me should I choose to make them my prey.

Even in my weakened state, they are no match for me.

I've lived for centuries on sheer will alone. I am the last of my kind—each one before me has been unwound by the dark magic our creator bestowed on us, and now their souls are lost in the ether, never to find refuge amongst the living or dead again. That will be my fate soon enough, but for now, I am trapped in this forsaken town.

It's filled with wretched people. Each one has committed more sins and discretions than I could keep track of. That's why I feel nothing when I kill them. Eating their dead had been a brief courtesy; now that I've tasted fresh blood, it will be all I hunger for while I remain here. At least in this pathetic land, there is no shortage of food. People in places like this go missing all the time, and no one ever comes looking for them.

That's why I'll drink my fill of their putrid blood—gorging myself on it until the endless hunger finally abates. That's all I am these days, an appetite. The depth of my starvation only grows. There is nothing beyond the empty void inside of me. It craves nothing but blood and bone and—*her*.

That woman with the red hair. It craves her, and I don't know why. It was foolish to let her escape. I should've drunk from her the same way I did that vile man.

However, as I linger in this dark alley, I can't regret my actions. How could I not have acted? That man would've harmed her. Killing him made her safe—and her safety is important to me. For reasons I don't understand.

I don't know what I expected—her to thank me? I huff a humorless laugh as I remember how she left screaming in terror and running for her life.

The same reaction everyone has when they see me if I don't devour them swiftly.

There had still been a part of me—a small, errant part that had hoped she would be different. That she would've...talked to me? A fresh wave of self-loathing washes over me. Perhaps this is the reason I'm the last of my kind. The rest of them had the good sense to be unwound while I'm out here wishing for things that can never be.

I am a monster. I will die alone, never having known true companionship.

Still, my mind won't forget the way she looked before she fled. The scarlet tendrils of her braided hair flowed down her back. She had wide, verdant eyes and the delicate freckles that decorated her pink cheeks. It made me wonder if she had freckles all over her. I had only caught faint traces of her rose scent on the wind. Still, it had been enough to make me wonder what her pale skin would feel like under my hands and if parts of her were softer than others.

The fantasy unravels from there. The idea that maybe she could want me under different circumstances. If I could call her mine, I would never let her go. I would keep her, protect her, and give her everything I could. I have never desired any living creature like this. It unsettles me as much as it intrigues me.

What would her flesh feel like against me? Against my tongue? She would burn hot enough to warm me every night as I held her to me. I would fall asleep with her in my arms and her rose scent invading my lungs. I would want nothing else.

But would she want me? I scoff at the question. Of course not. I am a death omen. My kind is solitary—she ran from me upon first sight, she would surely never welcome me into her bed.

I catch her scent on the breeze, luring me towards where she fled to. My body begs me to go—to follow it and lay claim to her. However, if I did that, I would be no better than the man who attacked her in the graveyard. Hurting her would be worse than never knowing what she felt like. Therefore, I will leave her in peace even as my desire for her grows.

I shake myself from those foolish thoughts. A dusting of fresh snow falls off my shoulder. How long have I been waiting out here? Too long. Just like I've been in this town for far too long. The sooner I leave here, the better. I'll drink my fill and then be gone—keeping my distance from her will be hard, but I must do it for both our sakes.

Finally, the tavern door bangs open on rusty hinges. An older man stumbles out, his gait uneven, clearly having indulged in his cups tonight. He will make for easy prey. Inhaling deeply, I scent the man's wretched soul. He's been here for some time, and he thinks he's escaped his past. The stain of his sins lingers in his blood—a murderer with countless victims who never atoned for his crimes.

Tonight, he will pay with his life.

Stalking silently behind him, I keep up with his pace down the barren streets. There is a gap between the buildings, and I strike. The man doesn't even scream before I drain him dry. The putrid taste of his blood eases my hunger and blocks out all other desires except for one.

I growl into his neck. One more day—that is it. I'll stay for one more day, drink as much as I can, and leave. If I am lucky, maybe I'll catch a glimpse of the red-headed woman before I have to say goodbye to her forever.

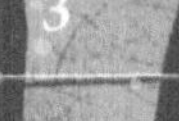

3

———

NORY

The sun dips closer to the horizon, bathing my front room in orange light.

Glancing at the clock, I see it is well past six o'clock in the evening. My mother converted the front portion of our house into a workstation soon after I started walking. It was easier for her to keep an eye on her sewing and her curious toddler if we were both confined to a single room.

Today had been particularly grueling. Four pairs of men's hunting trousers needed their inner seams redone. Two corsets needed to be reboned and their lacings replaced. Skirt hems, jackets with loose buttons, and disintegrating undergarments all found their way to me, and I tended to each one. My back aches as it always does after a particularly long day.

My fingers feel tight after having spent the day clutching onto my small needle—a dull throb pounds behind my eyes. Looking at the small stack of gold I made today for these orders, I wonder once more if this is all worth it. Being the only seamstress in town means there's always business, but the work is becoming too much for one person. After the expense of my mother's passing, I don't have enough to employ another seamstress.

The urge to shut my door and close shop is never more enticing than on days like today.

Part of me was grateful for the strenuous workload. It easily kept my mind off last night's events. However, now that my final customer has come to collect her things from me, knowing I will be alone makes unease trail icy fingers down my spine.

Collecting the freshly repaired stack of men's trousers, I hand them over to Isabelle. She smiles gratefully. While she may only be a few years older than me, she's been looking a bit worse for wear each time she comes to visit. Her once-bright golden hair has dulled to dishwater brown. The lines around her eyes and mouth have deepened.

The squeals of her children echo in from the porch. With three of them all under ten and at only twenty-seven, Isabelle must have her hands full. There is tiredness in her eyes, but something else too—a skittishness, one that replaced the good-natured young woman she used to be.

I know exactly who put that fear into her.

"Thank you, Nory," she says. "You always do such a wonderful job. Butch is always tearing holes in his pants. No better than a child, I say."

Even as she tries to laugh, there's a tightness to it. I don't miss how her eyes dart behind her as if her husband could have overheard her jibe.

"From all the hunting, yes?"

"Butch is a gifted hunter," Isabelle murmurs. "We are blessed that he has found such fortune in the forest."

I glance down at the state of her own clothes—the fraying at the top of her dress and the disastrous state of her soiled hem. Raising a brow, I nod at her.

"Are you sure you don't want me to fix your clothing? Or the children's?"

She comes to me nearly once a week, always in the same drab garments. The children are no better with their hole-ridden boots and pants two sizes too small.

Isabelle's lips turn down, a sad smile overtaking her face.

"Quite sure. I only have enough coins to pay for Butch."

I open my mouth, wanting so badly to tell her what everyone in town thinks of her husband. He is a miser. Squirreling away the large sums of gold he makes from each of his plentiful hunts, using those coins to satisfy himself in deplorable ways. Gambling, drinking, adultery—there isn't a sin her husband hasn't partaken in.

Meanwhile, Isabelle toils away as a maid in some of the wealthier families' homes. The children live on her meager salary while their father spends his gold as he pleases. He cares little for his children—even less so for his wife. There is no way Isabelle is ignorant of the sordid stories told about her husband.

The man disgusts me, but he is far from the only horrible one in this town. That is why I hold my tongue. What good would it be to tell Isabelle what I thought? I would hate for her to think I was another gossip who talked about her misfortunes behind her back. She is a kind woman who's been through enough.

Silence stretches between us for a moment, both clearly wanting to say more but deciding it is unwise. Reaching into her pocket, she grips a small coin purse and holds it towards me. At the motion, the worn sleeve of her dress pulls back, revealing a reddish purple bruise. The unsightly mark encases her entire wrist.

I gasp, my eyes widening as they meet hers. Isabelle's hand begins to tremble, and unshed tears pool in her brown eyes. Glancing over her shoulder, she once again confirms that Butch has not magically appeared at my threshold.

"He's been so awful lately," Isabelle whispers. "More awful

than ever before. His drinking is worse. It used to be his yelling we would have to endure, but now..."

A shiver causes her whole frail body to convulse.

"I'm worried he'll start hurting the children. I can endure it, but them—I could not live with myself if they bore the brunt of his anger. My youngest is barely two, I don't want him raised in fear."

"Leave him," I say. "Surely there is someone who would take you in."

Isabelle's small smile returns as tears fall down her cheeks.

"There is nowhere for us to go. Despite keeping his money from us, he does provide us with food and shelter. I could never support three children on my own. We would surely perish without him." A bitter laugh escapes her. "The only way we'd ever be free of him was if he died, but I'm not naive enough to hope for a hunting accident to save us."

I open my mouth to respond, but Isabelle drops the sack of coins on my work table with a thud.

"Thank you again, Nory. Don't worry about us, we will make it through. Somehow, we always find a way."

Without another word, Isbaelle scoops up her husband's clothes and turns to leave.

Even though she told me not to, I can't help but worry about her, especially as I watch her collect her three children who have been waiting on the stoop. They are all dressed poorly, a far cry from the sturdy garments I fixed for their father. The eldest is a girl of nearly eight. Her golden hair is hidden beneath a white cap. Taking each of her younger brother's hands, she glances over her shoulder, and our eyes meet through the window.

Her brown irises are wide and beseeching. While they may be fed and have a place to sleep at night, what kind of life are they truly living? One ruled by fear at the hands of their drunkard father. Time only makes men like him worse.

The Snowlands encourage the worst amongst us to give in to their depraved natures. Their dark souls fester until all those around them are forced to suffer. If only there were something I could do to help them—if only there were someone who could stop men like Butch from hurting their families.

Lord Gunnar was meant to keep order, but he is just as rotten as the rest of the men here. Or was. *Was.* Someone saved me from my horrible fate.

An idea sparks—a wild and forbidden idea, but once it is there, I cannot unthink it. Glancing across the front yard, the last rays of the evening sun paint the horizon in purples and pinks. If that creature had any sense, he would've left town by now, but if he hasn't...there's still a chance.

My mother would be turning in her grave if she knew what I planned to do. She was a spiritual woman in many ways—ways the people in this town didn't understand. In her vast knowledge of herbal remedies and protection charms, she taught me how to do something out of caution. Only in the most desperate of situations was I meant to perform this ritual.

The situation seemed desperate to me, and there was no time to waste. The light was fading fast, and I had a monster to summon.

Snatching up my small bag of coins, I collect my cloak and stare out into the darkening night.

"What do I have to lose?"

WHAT I HAVE to lose turns out to be a handful of coins and a few drops of my blood.

I pray the wound won't get infected as I stow my danger and watch the crimson pour from my hand and dot the top of the coins piled atop my mother's grave. With her nearby, I feel protected. Even if I can practically hear her screaming from the beyond at how reckless I'm being.

There's no turning back now. With a deep breath, I close my eyes and recite the words taught to me by my mother.

"Come to me, he who dwells amongst the living. Come to me, he who was born amongst the dead. Come to me, he who will shepherd me at my end."

Silence follows after my last word. Even the breeze seems to cease blowing. A fresh dusting of snow coats the sparse grass beneath my feet. My breathing is the only sound in this still graveyard.

Then an icy wind blows over me, nearly knocking me to the ground. I manage to withstand it somehow. My heart hammers painfully in my chest. Even without opening my eyes, I know I am no longer alone. His presence overwhelms me. My instincts to run flood my body, but I remain still. This is why I came here —to strike a deal with a demon.

Peeling open my eyes, I am greeted by the gruesome sight from the night before. Glowing eyes stare at me from deep inside his skull. His hood is up, protecting his waxy skin from the flurries in the air. The long cloak is sprawled out behind him like spilled ink.

"I must admit," he says, voice like a death rattle. "It's been an age since someone has summoned me."

His eyes narrow, the bluish glow inside them intensifying.

"You must be even more foolish than I thought."

I open my mouth but find I have no voice. Trepidation has stolen it from me. I thought I could withstand the sight of him, but every instinct I have is begging me to run. Fear spears claws into my stomach. I'm trembling but not from the cold. I must steady myself and keep my wits about me. One wrong move and I'm done for. I need to play my hand perfectly for my plan to work.

The revenant does not give me a chance to think, however. In a flash, he is before me, nearly making me stumble back. With a swipe of his bony hand, he snatches up the coins atop my mother's grave, healing them where his nose should be. With a growl, he sucks the gold into his mouth, licking my blood from them with relish. The glow in his eyes nearly forcing me to look away.

He spits the now clean coins into his palm before tucking them away. Before I'm aware of his movement, I feel a cool hand wrap around my wrist. Bringing my injured palm towards his mouth, I watch his strong jaw unhinge and his purple tongue sneak out. My stomach tightens as I watch it lick up the inside of my palm. The warm, wet glide of it sends tingles through my body. It is not an unpleasant feeling.

The revelation wakes me from whatever fear-induced stupor I was in. Snatching my hand back, I glare at him. An unwise thing to do, but I do not take kindly to anyone licking me without permission—man or monster. Glancing down at my hand, I expect to find he's marred me in some way, but all I see is uninjured skin.

He has magic, something I knew, but now it's been confirmed.

The revenant licks his pale lips, his skin growing more opaque. A deep chuckle leaves him as he stares down at me.

"What is it you want from me, human?"

His voice is soft and rough at the same time. Planting my feet firmly on the ground, and meeting his intense gaze with one of my own.

"For us to come to some sort of arrangement. If you will—"

He cuts me off with a wave of his hand.

"I don't bargain with humans. I'm not that kind of demon." He snatches my wrist again, tugging me closer. "Even if you are delicious."

Warmth erupts on my cheeks, but I still manage to thrash in his grip.

"Then you are wasting my time," I spit, trying to dislodge myself.

His grip on me never falters. Instead, he stares down at me with a bemused expression. That enrages me even more. He is not willing to help me, and now he is keeping me against my will. I fight against him, but it is of no use.

The creature chuckles again before shaking his head.

"I can't remember the last time I've been amused. Quite a novel feeling." He pulls me closer, our bodies nearly touching. "Go on, tiny human. Tell me why you've summoned me."

With a deep sigh, I cease my struggling. This is my one chance to get what I need from him. Mother always warned me that creatures like him were fickle and their amusement could turn into annoyance in an instant. I should take advantage of his goodwill while I have it.

"There is a woman in town—she and her children are suffering greatly at the hands of her wretched husband." I lick my lips. "If you would agree to help me, I could lure him out for you, and you could kill him just as you did Lord Gunnar last night."

The revenant's face twists, and I hold my breath, waiting for him to decide he's heard enough and chooses to make a meal out of me instead.

"If devouring that disgusting man last night has given you the impression that I'm some sort of undead vigilante, then you have the entirely wrong opinion about me, human." I lower my brows as he presses on. "And what would my reward be for aiding you in dispatching this man? His festering blood—rotten from his putrid soul."

I can't hide my cringe. "Well, yes—I have some gold if you would like that as payment instead."

The creature's eyes roam over me. I feel his burning gaze

like a caress. It's different from the way Gunnar would look at me. My reaction to it is different as well. I don't dislike how it makes me feel—I don't want to hide from him. I must have truly lost my mind. First, I summoned a demon, and now I am letting him gaze at me with unbridled wanting. The urge to flee is also suspiciously missing the longer I stare back at him.

Licking his lips, his eyes blaze red.

"What about you?"

My body becomes warm and heavy. Without his grip on me, I know I would collapse to the ground in a puddle.

"What about me?" My voice sounds rough to my own ears.

The revevant skims his finger up my wrist, digging softly into my pulse point.

"The only way I'd be tempted to enter into this arrangement with you is if you offered me your blood as payment."

A gasp puffs from between my lips.

"I—I don't wish to die."

Despite my desire to save Isabelle and her children, I don't want to relinquish my own life for it. The revevant merely chuckles, his hand on my wrist moving higher, dancing between my own.

"It would be a waste to drain you dry in one go. I can savor it —savor you."

His hand ghosts over my cheek before falling away.

"Still," he says, "despite how tempting you are, I would require more than just your blood to satisfy me. Especially if there are others you wish to aid through our partnership."

My cheeks warm at his assertion. "I hadn't mentioned helping others."

"But you would," he says. "I tasted it in your blood—if I agreed to your terms, you'd seek me out to help all those you deem worthy of it. A noble feat—one I will indulge should I be compensated in a way I see fitting."

My tongue suddenly feels too large in my mouth. Feelings

I've never had before swirl inside me, encouraging my body to warm. I should be quick to deny what he wants—to tell him this was a mistake and that I am certainly not on offer.

I do nothing of the sort and am startled to realize that I am considering his proposition. However, I must make certain of what he is asking before I agree.

"Speak plainly, what is it that you demand of me?"

I sound breathless. The revevant is quiet in contemplation for a moment. His eyes continue their slow descent from my head to my chest. Lingering in my places that make my heart speed up.

"Companionship," he says finally.

His request is odd enough to give me pause. He must read the confusion on my face as he presses on.

"I have been a solitary creature all my life. Created alone in *The Woods* by my maker, I survived on the blood of animals until I grew old enough to wander. Once I was mature in body and magic, I travelled this world as a seeking appetite, my only motivation was to satiate the hunger inside of me." His eyes burn, and I feel the warmth on my face. "Over the centuries, I've grown envious of your kind. Your bonds, your closeness."

His hand returns to my face, skimming over my cheek. The breath in my lungs still, and I'm left reeling. Shockingly enough, I find myself leaning into his touch. Whatever magic he wields, he is surely using it on me now. I cannot control my body or the response he elicits from it. This must be some sort of trick.

Mustn't it?

The waxy softness of his skin envelopes my cheek. The slight touch makes me hot and aching all over.

"Your warmth calls to me," he sighs. "If you wish for my help, you must give yourself to me—freely and willingly."

"Are you," I pause, biting my lower lip. "That is to say, are you not using magic on me now?"

The revevant's eyes burn, and his hand on my cheek tightens.

"No."

Shock renders me silent for a few moments. He could be lying, but he has no reason to. It is a dizzying revelation that my body is acting this way towards him because I want it to. There is some part of me that wants him in a way I never had another. My mind whirls, the world beneath my feet tilts.

"What—what does that mean entirely? I've never been with a man." Fire erupts in my cheeks, and I drop his gaze. "Let alone a—"

"A monster," he offers.

His hand drops from my face, and his gaze cools. There is suddenly a wall between us, and I don't like it. My hand itches to take hold of his, but I resist the urge. It seems my mind and heart conflict with one another.

"I already knew this about you," he sighs. "Countless men of this town have met their end between my lips, and more than a fair share of them had had thoughts about you—lecherous ones. I tasted the desire flowing in their putrid blood. None of them more so than the worm I drank from last night."

His confession makes my blood run cold. Sure, I've caught the wandering eye of a few men in town, but I never thought they would have designs on me. Let alone such deplorable thoughts—bile races up my throat.

"When the news of that foul lord's death spreads, they will come searching for you now that his claim is gone. Each one with their own agendas." His eyes blaze a searing white light. "I will protect you from them, so long as you agree to be mine."

Agree to be his.

The declaration settles into the marrow of my bones. I'm not ignorant of what some of the men in town think of me. In some ways, Lord Gunnar was protecting me, and his claim on me had kept the vultures away. With him gone, there is no such safeguard, and some will not take my refusals as he had. I am very much in danger.

Unless I accept the revenant's proposal.

"I will not force myself upon you," he says, relieving some of my worries. "I merely want closeness. Warmth. To share a bed with you. To hold you while you sleep and to dine at the same table."

It sounds simple enough—there are parts of me that desire the same thing even if my mind cannot make sense of it. I would be a fool to deny his protection and his aid in helping Isabelle's situation. Still, I can't help but question him.

"Why is this what you desire? You could demand anything from me."

The revevant shrugs, his cloak flowing in the soft breeze.

"My time in this world is drawing shorter—each day is a battle to stay tethered here. I want to experience true companionship before it's too late."

My heart squeezes painfully in my chest.

"Why?" I whisper. "Why with me?"

The creature's eyes blaze scarlet, and his hand reaches for me again. I hold my breath at the contact. His gaze turns gentle as it traces over my face.

"You are the most beautiful woman I have ever seen. With the most delicious blood I have ever tasted. Never in all my centuries have I wanted anything as much as I want you."

I suck in a breath. Confusion swirls within me at his earnest declaration. I do not fear him—not as I did last night. He will not harm me in the way Lord Gunnar had planned, or many of the men in the Snowlands would surely do given the chance. If it is companionship he wants, then that's what I'll provide.

Have I not been feeling lonely as well? Are we really so different him and I?

Without giving myself time to reconsider, I nod into his hand.

"I will agree to your terms, revenant," I say. His hand on my face flexes. "If you agree to aid me in my plan and keep me safe, I will give myself to you freely and willingly."

A slow grin spreads across his face. It makes me shiver—not in fear but with rampant desire. He looks different when he smiles—less monstrous. The curve to his mouth is all male satisfaction as his hand slides from my cheek and falls down the back of my cloak. I allow him to pull me into him.

"There is only one way to seal our deal."

With a nod, I know what he wants without even asking. I tip my head back and stare up at the glowing moon. The stars twinkle down at us as the cold night air stings my nose. Snowflakes collect on my lashes. I shiver, and it has nothing to do with the temperature and everything to do with the feel of his massive body enveloping me.

"Tell me your name," he commands.

"Nory," I sigh as I feel his tongue skim up the column of my throat.

He murmurs my name against my skin as if savoring the taste.

"I'm Eryx."

His cheek skims against mine, and I gasp. His lips press softly against my throat where he just licked, and my knees turn to jelly. Without warning, I feel a sharp bite of pain, and then euphoria erupts inside of me. The soft sound of him sucking at my neck washes over me. There is only him and me. His earthy pine scent wraps around me and suffocates me. My body heats and clenches in places I didn't know were possible.

I need more—I need everything from him. I could die like this and have no regrets. All I feel now is warm and complete. I tremble in his grasp, my body racing towards an unknown peak. The spot between my thighs grows achy, and I am desperate for any sort of relief.

With a broken growl piercing my ears, I finally feel him pull away. The wet slide of his tongue along my throat closes whatever wound he caused and breaks the spell I was under. My breathing is ragged as if I've just run a great distance without stopping. I look up at him.

I let out a whimper as he licks my blood from his lips.

"So, Nory. When shall we begin?" he asks.

The first part of my mission has been accomplished; hopefully, this next part will go off without a hitch. Blinking through my heavy eyelids, I find his hand and take it in my own.

"Right now."

4

———

ERYX

Feeling more foolish than I ever have in my life, I wait where the little human instructed me to.

Cloaked in shadow, in the alley across from the noisy tavern, I lie in wait. It has begun snowing in earnest, and little white piles have built up atop my shoulders. It's the only indication of how long I've been waiting out here. Not for the first time since I felt her summons tonight, I question exactly what I am doing. I am a fool.

If I had any sense at all, I'd turn from this tavern—this town, this woman—and never look back. Why would I agree to such an arrangement with what little time I have left?

I know the answer. It's her—Nory—the small human with a bewitching face and delicious blood. Through the foggy tavern windows, I can just see her. She's sitting at one of the long bar tables with a forgotten mug of ale in front of her.

The long tresses of her red hair match the maddening red gown she has on. Indecent only because of the way it highlights her creamy skin. I hadn't understood her need to get it from her cottage, and yet I had waited outside for her to change like a dutiful servant before we made our way into town. The window blurs most of her face, save for those bewitching green eyes.

Her movements are soft as she shyly looks around the bar. It is all an act. I've seen the defiance in her gaze—how she fights against her fear for what she wants.

I no longer scare her; that was made clear in the graveyard. It was a revelation to watch her lean into my touch and even more shocking when she reached for me of her own accord.

When was the last time someone willingly touched me? Never, if I had to guess. Nory is the first and, assuredly, the only one. I watch her intently through the window. Can she not tell just how badly the male patrons hunger after her?

I can hardly blame them. I too cannot resist the temptation she inspires within me. She is mine—to protect, to serve for as long as I live in this between state—neither dead nor alive. She makes me feel alive, though. As if I'm burning by the force of a thousand suns, my lust for her rages inside of me.

Just as it had raged inside the men I've drained all over the Snowlands. She had consumed each of their waking thoughts —a veritable siren of these forsaken lands. No one's thoughts had been more depraved than the man I killed in front of her— something I would do a thousand times over.

It was a privilege to protect her. Even though I was a fool to reveal myself to her, I cannot regret doing so. I was not strong enough to remain hidden, for she has bewitched me just as she has the others of this town. Where she goes, I will helplessly follow. That is why I will fulfill my promise to help her in exchange for her companionship.

Truth be told, I would've helped her had she not agreed, I am that powerless when it comes to her.

I cannot deny the pleasure I feel at her acceptance of my terms. It was a childish fantasy—but one I have held onto for years. I am a solitary wanderer. The last of my kind was unwound decades ago. The dark magic that stitches us all together had been severed, and each of their souls had been cast into the void, leaving behind husks where their bodies should be. The same fate awaits me, with each day creeping closer. I've felt my time dwindling for a while now. My magic has weakened, and my hunger refuses to be satiated.

That is why this is my last chance to feel something other than hunger before it's too late. I hadn't expected her to be merciful and agree. Whoever it is we are helping must be dear to her. That or Nory is uncommonly kind and brave.

My eyes lock onto a figure that has come near her in the tavern. I watch her posture change, still shy but more open, as if relieved to see this person. He settles in across from her, and a smile tugs on her full lips. Through the foggy glass, I can make out the tightness around her mouth. It's her only tell that this shy disposition is all an act.

Pulling my eyes away from Nory is no easy feat, but somehow I manage to. I survey the man across from her. A glass of amber liquid is clenched in his meaty fist. His dark hair is pulled back in a low bun at the top of his neck. His clothes are immaculate if a little worn at the knees—a cloak lined with gray wolf's fur lounges on his shoulders.

The man is massive. His impressive chest rises and falls quickly. Even sitting down, he towers over Nory's petite frame. The man's gaze is burning with intensity. His dark eyes travel down her in one lustful stroke.

I cannot read minds word for word, but I can sense energies and intentions. This man's desire could not be more singularly focused. The sight makes my teeth grind. While I cannot blame the other male, I do not like it. I pray this is her target, and I will take great pleasure in ending his life between my jaws.

My eyes return to Nory, who giggles softly. The neckline of her scarlet gown pulls lower, highlighting the swells of her breasts. The man notices, licking his lips in earnest. He leans closer over the table and says something that causes her to blush into her mug of ale.

Nory nods to him once before rising gracefully and smoothing out the front of her gown. She tucks a piece of her hair behind her ear before looking away. The bashfulness is all an act. This pretend skittish creature would never summon a monster like me and demand my help. This must be her plan—her ploy. Get this male to lower his guard enough to follow her wherever she wishes. Then, at the right moment, I will act and end his sorry existence.

Slipping from the table, Nory smiles at him before nodding towards the door. I watch as she takes her cloak and slides through the tavern door quietly. Slowly, she begins walking over towards where I am hidden in the alley. My eyes return to the man watching as he grins, downs the rest of his liquor in one gulp, and lurches to his feet. The tavern door bangs open loudly as he pushes through it.

Nory's sweet scent of roses reaches me, her eyes and mine connecting for a moment. She opens her mouth, but before she can get a word out, the stench of alcohol blights her smell. In an instant, the man has reached her, his hands wrapping around her waist and pulling her into him. She gasps as he deftly backs her into the closest alley wall. His head falls to her shoulder, inhaling greedily—lips moving against her flesh.

"I knew you always wanted me, knew it from the looks you'd give me around town. Don't worry, no one will know. This will be our little secret," the man slurs against her.

Nory's face morphs into one of disgust as she pushes at his shoulder. He is much larger than her—her resistance isn't even registering. My teeth grind together as his pale tongue licks up her throat in the same spot mine had—red mists over my vision, and my magic hums to life. Nory's eyes blaze as they lock with mine.

"Now," she mouths, and I strike.

A snarl echoes in the quiet alley as I move on swift, silent feet. My hands wrap around the man and pull him from her. Even in his drunken state, the man has the good sense to look shocked. He pushes against me, but it is useless. He is my prey now, and I have him pinned to the wall in an instant. My *lifefire* blazes inside of me, reaching an inferno. I am burning everywhere, and I will channel it all into ending this man.

I snarl into his purpling face, my grip on his throat cutting off his air supply.

"You will die for touching her. For your vile actions and wretched life that has brought pain to all those around you, you will die alone and in fear."

The scent of urine coats the air, and I chuckle darkly. Unhinging my jaw, I let him see the monster I genuinely am. All remaining color leeches from his face. His fear tastes bitter, but the hunger inside of me doesn't mind. My teeth embed themselves in his throat and drink down his blood. The sticky warmth is tangy—poisoned with his rotten soul. The man struggles against me, but it is useless.

Especially when I bite into his neck and rip out his throat muscles, spitting the flesh onto the ground with a wet thud, he begins bleeding in earnest now. Once the man goes limp in my grasp, I let his body fall onto the hard ground. His eyes are open but unfocused. Blood coats the snowy grass beneath him. My breathing is ragged as I take in the sight, the high from the feeding still coursing through my veins.

A gasp from behind me startles me into awareness. I whirl from the bloody sight and take in Nory. She has gone pale, her whole body trembling as she stares up at me. I clean my face with a tattered sleeve and prowl towards her. Unease dances in my stomach.

"I didn't know I would feel like this," Nory whimpers.

Her knees begin to buckle, but before she hits the ground, I catch her in my arms. I hold her close, absorbing her warmth and waiting for her to push me away.

"You made a pact with a death omen. If you regret our deal, tell me now, and this will be done."

Of course, she would be disgusted by me. Now that she has seen what I am truly capable of, there is no possibility of her welcoming me into her bed, her heart. I was foolish to think otherwise. I wait for her rejection, hoping that it comes swiftly so that I may save a bit of my pride.

Scarlet lashes flutter atop her freckled cheeks. Her green eyes swirl with an emotion I've never seen before. Slowly, she reaches up, and her warm palm cradles my cheek.

"That is not what I meant," she sighs. "I didn't know watching him die would make me feel this...this *happy*."

The world around me freezes. She licks her lower lip as her eyes unfocus.

"I liked watching him die. I shouldn't admit that—but I did. He was a wretched man who hurt his wife and children. Who would've hurt me had you not been here." Her hand on my cheek tightens. "I'm glad he's gone. It makes me—it makes me want—"

"Yes?" My hand rests atop hers on my face, savoring her soft skin.

"To do it again," she says finally.

The world around me spins, and for a moment, I believe I have already been unwound, and instead of the void, I have been granted the privilege of heaven. Though even as I think that, I know it cannot be true. The bitter air around me still swirls, as does the rasping air in my lungs. Nory's floral scent envelopes me with its sweetness. I am still alive, and I thank my maker for their kindness.

The heat in Nory's bright eyes is familiar to me, for it is the same desire I have in my gaze for her. Never in a dozen centuries would I ever consider her looking at me like this—

with yearning. To have her want me—a wretched, disgusting creature—is a gift I am not worthy of.

That is why every day that I remain in this world, I will live for her in whatever capacity I can. If only to keep her looking at me like that.

"Tell me who's next. I'll kill them all for you, I swear it."

Nory's pink lips transform into a wide smile—a real one this time, where no unease pinches the sides.

"One is more than enough for tonight," she says. "I'll need to choose our next target wisely."

Her hand leaves my cheek to slide behind my neck. I groan as the supple curves of her body press into me. Her soft laugh is the sweetest music I have ever heard. Tucking herself firmly against me, her smile widens.

"Until then, take me home, Eryx." Her lips press close to my ear. "It's time for me to hold up my end of the bargain."

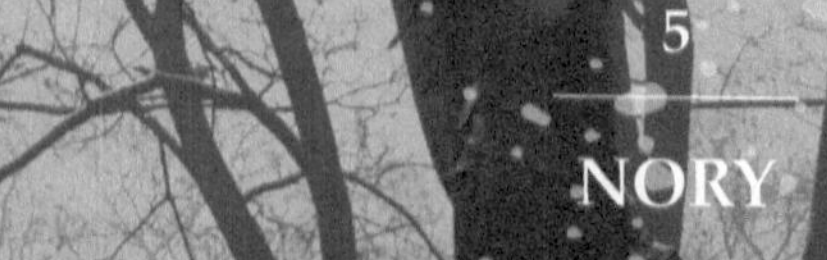

I t doesn't take long for us to arrive back at the cottage.

Eryx's footsteps creak on the old wooden porch. The cold wind whips at my unbound hair and stings my cheeks. Sliding out of his arms, I immediately miss the warmth of his body. Part of me still feels a little off-kilter.

My plan tonight had gone off without a hitch.

Butch was a more than eager participant, as I knew he would be. It took barely a few minutes of conversation before I had him agreeing to meet me in the alley. I can still feel his hands on my body—smell the stench of whiskey on his breath as his seeking mouth found purchase on my flesh. A shiver rocks me, and I push the unsavory memories aside.

He'll be discovered soon enough, and Isabelle and her children will finally be free. I don't regret my actions. Nor do I care that I brought forth his demise. In fact, I like the hand I played in all of it—far more than I should. I couldn't help but feel a sense of relief watching Eryx drain the life from him.

One less evil man is prowling the streets thanks to us.

Finding my keys tucked into the pocket of my cloak, I turn the lock and relish in the familiar click—the old door swings open on groaning hinges, revealing the front room of my house. I can't help the burning on my cheeks as I take in the disastrous sight.

"You'll have to excuse the mess." I step over the worn threshold and deftly kick a stack of fraying trousers out of the walkway. "There's been no shortage of mendings lately."

In this moment, I'm acutely aware of the fact that in my twenty-four years of life, I've never had a visitor over. The only people ever in this room besides my mother and me were customers. Now, I see it through the eyes of a stranger. The workroom is a riot of different fabrics. The long wooden work table is weighed down with piles of half-fixed garments.

My needles with their string tails lay strewn across the scuffed mahogany. Five wardrobes line the walls with their doors removed, showcasing the overflowing dresses hanging inside. Shifts and stockings lay across the back of an old velvet loveseat. I'm overwhelmed by the chaos—at the notion that I've been living like this for so long, I hadn't even taken notice.

The only kept area is the small, tidy area along the far wall near the hearth. There lies a sparse bookshelf and an untouched set of chairs arranged around a small circular table. It was meant for meals, but Mother and I always took ours at the work table or ate right in the kitchen.

"I'll start a fire. The chill may not be bad yet, but it'll get worse throughout the night." For some reason, I can't bear to face him, so I busy myself with other tasks. "There is a small kitchen in the back. A staircase, too, that leads to the bedrooms on the second floor."

I'm not surprised by the silence that greets me. He's probably appalled at the mess, which seems ridiculous—he's a revenant after all—but perhaps they're neat creatures. The state of his armour and cloak says other ways, but you never know. Speaking of cloaks, I'm itching to take mine off.

Once the fire is roaring and warmth washes over me, I

quickly shed my cloak and hang it beside the hearth to dry. The brilliant scarlet fabric of the dress blazes in the firelight. I would never usually wear such a garment—the only reason I have it is because a farmer's wife paid my mother to take it off her hands a few years ago. The woman's husband had said it was a sin to wear such a color.

It had been just what I needed tonight, though.

Usually, I stick to drab colors—not only because the fabric is cheaper, but also because attracting too much attention in the Snowlands can be dangerous. There is safety in remaining unseen, especially as a single woman. I had attracted Lord Gunnar's attention, and look how that nearly panned out.

However, I am not alone now. No, I have given myself to a creature—a monster I've watched kill two men right in front of me. *Not a monster,* I silently correct myself, *Eryx—his name is Eryx.*

The only living being besides my mother who's ever looked out for me. And who's been suspiciously quiet since we've arrived.

Turning from the fire, my eyes land on the figure standing just beyond the door. His pale hand is braced on the doorframe. The glow in his eyes has dimmed, and he remains fixed on me. Why has he not come in? If the mess in the room is off-putting to him, he hardly seems to notice.

The intensity of his gaze causes my heart to pound as we continue to stare at each other. After a moment, he shakes himself. The tattered ends of his cloak kiss the door jam.

"You must invite me in," he rasps, answering my unspoken question. "My magic is fickle and comes with many cumbersome rules."

"Oh," I say, blushing once more. "Of course—come in, please."

His hulking frame prowls through the open door. He has to stoop down in order not to hit his head on the top of the door.

Each decisive step makes his armor rattle softly. The ends of his cloak drag across the wooden floors in a whisper of rustling fabric.

The door slams shut behind him, followed by a sharp click of the lock. A metallic scent dances in the air as a reminder of the magical being I've given myself to during the duration of this bargain.

Heat from the fire continues to warm me to the point I feel sweat gliding down my spine. The air around me shifts—turning charged in an instant. It's not long before I realize this heat kindling in my body has nothing to do with the fire. It has everything to do with the Eryx as he approaches me. Power exudes from him and dances over my body. The fire in his gaze makes me feel naked in my tight dress, and for the first time in my life, I don't fear this type of look.

Still, I can't help but cross my arms over my chest to cover the hardening of my nipples. My body has never responded to another in this way, but no other has ever made me feel the way Eryx has. He has awakened something in me I thought would lie dormant for all time.

His eyes glow in the firelight. The shadows of his face deepen as I watch him scent the air. Eryx's body drifts closer to mine, and I feel his cloak brush against my booted feet. The scent of night and soil flows into my lungs.

"Are you hungry?" I ask, trying to ease the tension between us somehow. "I have stew—day-old bread that should have kept well. I can—"

"You know very well what sustains me." His voice is a low growl.

My mouth goes dry. The world around me spins, and I once again question if I'm not under some spell. I've scented his magic before, and I know it isn't at play here. I was of sound mind when I struck the bargain—just as I am of sound mind now. These new revelations have left me reeling, but my curiosity has overcome any sort of trepidation. It's how I manage to find my voice.

"And are you hungry for that?" I swallow. "For...*me?*"

His eyes blaze bright. His skin takes on a new sheen, glistening. He raises a hand and it ghosts over my cheek, making my breath catch. The featherlight touch makes my whole body prickle with awareness. The space between my thighs turns wet —needy, seeking. I have to bite my lip to keep from crying out.

"For centuries, I have lived only as an insatiable appetite." His fingers play with a lock of my hair. "Yet never have I ever hungered for anything the way I do for you."

My arms fall away from my chest as I drift closer to him. The cold, rigid plates of his armor press against my aching nipples, and I bite back a moan. Eryx hisses at the contact. I should be fearful of him—he is a creature from my worst nightmares. Instead, all I feel is curious. In his gaze, I can see him so plainly.

This is a lonely creature. Eryx has only known solidarity and instant gratification after gorging himself on blood and corpses. That is no true existence. I can see the male he longs to be simmering in his eyes, and I can give that to him. Despite his desire for blood, we are not so different. I have been adrift in my own lonely existence.

It would be nice to find companionship with another, even if he just so happens to be a revenant. He protected me, helped me—how many men in this village would've done the same? They would've hurt me the first chance they got. Not Eryx. I believe he'd sooner harm himself than bring about my discomfort.

I trust him—enough to let the last of my inhibition fade at least for tonight.

Extending my hand towards him, I find the tie of his cloak and pull it free. The old fabric drops into an unkempt heap. Without it, the shiny plates of his armor sparkle. Sinew muscles are coiled beneath the metal, and I long to see him fully unclothed. Not yet, though.

Cupping his cheek, my thumb digs into the hollow there. I've never touched a man like this before. We are in uncharted territory, and I relinquish myself to it.

"Feed from me." My voice is steady and clear. "Have me."

The fire in his eyes reaches a blazing peak. Eryx understands my meaning. I want him to find completion not just from my blood but my body as well. I want to tease out this more fragile side to him. I want to be with the male who only asked for companionship from me—I want to free him from whatever is holding him back.

More than that, I want to free myself too. I've been cautious for too long. I will not live the rest of my life in fear. Not when wanton desire flows through my veins and causes wetness to seep from my most feminine flesh.

His thin fingers tease the column of my throat.

"Your blood calls to me. But that is not all I want."

Fingertips kiss my jaw before tickling my lower lip. A moan works its way up my throat.

"Watching that man tonight—the way he looked at you, the vile thoughts he had—filled me with more anger than I can ever remember having." His eyes burn me alive. "It was a delight to kill him—to know he will never touch you again. He will never do you harm. Before I leave this place, I will slaughter anyone who thinks to take from you what you will not give."

"I will give you whatever you wish from me."

My confession is a broken whisper and shocks both of us— Eryx's hand cups my face, the lines of his body tight as if holding himself back. I want him freed—unleashed upon me in whatever way he wants.

"Take what you want from me, for I have never longed for another the way I long for you. I cannot explain it. I—"

"You must be some final offering," he interjects. "Some kind of goddess, sent to bestow a final favor on a wretched creature."

"Eryx—"

"I just wish to hold you close," he groans, and I fall against him. "To taste your sweet lips—for yours to be the only ones I've ever known before the magic unmakes me."

Unmakes him? The statement unsettles me. The thought of my time with Eryx being limited makes me even more determined to throw caution to the wind. I give in to my delirious need for him. I rub myself against his hard body. My thighs clench, desperate for some friction.

Wrapping my arms around his neck, I press up onto my toes and finally meet my mouth with his. It is a chaste touch. Both our movements are unpracticed—the last kiss I bestowed on anyone was on a farmer's son when I was sixteen. This kiss is much better than that, even if it is unrefined.

The soft skin of his lips is warm against mine. My whole body trembles as a fresh wave of pleasure washes over me. Pulling back, I stare up into his fiery eyes and nearly melt. Lust lies bare in his gaze, as does another more equally powerful emotion. My body heats more from the look he's giving me than the fire we stand before.

With a growl permeating his chest, he pulls me back into his embrace, and our mouths connect again. This time, our kiss is a savage one. It is a meeting of skin and a clashing of lips. His hands smooth over my back before rising higher and finding the sleeves of my gown. His fingers slip underneath the fabric and pull down. Lowering my arms, I help him free more of my skin until only the top of my shift and corset cover my breasts. My nipples pebble behind the stiff fabric, begging me to free them to his hungry gaze.

As if reading my mind, his deft hands fall to the lacing of my corset and undo the ties. Again, his movements are novice, and that only makes me want him more. To know I'm the only one he's touched in this way makes my head spin, and I kiss him back more forcefully. We're both breathing heavy by the time my corset falls to the floor.

I gasp into his mouth as his hands drag along my back. In only my shift, it feels as if he's touching my bare skin. The slow, wet glide of his tongue against my lips causes me to tremble. I open for him and allow his seeking muscle to find its way between my lips. He tastes of night air and smoke. The faint metallic taste of blood lingers on his tongue, encouraging my desire instead of tainting it.

We moan as our tongues twin together in a sloppy battle for dominance. The more we kiss, the more we learn to understand each other. Soon we find our rhythm—tasting, biting, and breathing in each other's scents—his hand slides down my back and cups my ass. Eryx pulls me flush against him, and behind the soft material of his pants, not covered in armour, I discover a new hardness. One I've only felt in sickening moments by men I abhor.

Now, I feel that hot, seeking length, and my knees nearly buckle. More moisture slicks out of me, eager to have that piece of him deep inside of me. I rub my stomach back and forth against it, smiling broadly at his resulting hiss.

His lips leave mine, and I'm immediately wishing for them back.

"My beautiful tormentor," he whispers in my ear. "Too delicious for your own good."

"Eryx," I moan as his lips travel down.

He lays kisses against my jaw. Removing his hands from my backside, they travel around to my front and gently palm my aching breasts through my shift. I tilt my head back as he teases each one. Testing their weight before working my nipples with his thumb. I rub my thighs together as my moans engulf us.

Eryx's lips travel down the column of my throat. There, he licks in time with his teasing fingers. I feel the press of his teeth, but the nip isn't hard enough to break skin. My hands fall to the back of his head, encouraging him.

"Bite me," I beg, desperate to have him drink from me again.

His hands still on my breasts before breaking off on a groan.

"Sweet, merciful goddess," he sighs into my neck.

Without another word, I feel the sharp prick of pain. Then, nothing but euphoria wraps around me. Pleasure dances on every nerve ending and envelopes me. The sound of him drinking from my neck heightens my arousal. My body races towards an invisible peak. Wetness coats my inner thighs as he continues to drink from me. Every muscle in my body pulls tight as he takes his fill and then—*snap.*

I am lost to my climax. Euphoria erupts inside of me, and sticky, sweet pleasure coats me. My eyes are open, yet I see nothing. There is only Eryx—only the feel of him at my neck and his hands holding me steady. Without him, my limp muscles wouldn't support me.

Sweet bliss makes my body tremble with fleeting pleasure.

Vaguely, I am aware of Eryx pulling away from me. His warm tongue glides up my neck to seal his bite wound. His gaze is on mine, and concern is etched on it—as if worried that I will turn away from him. As if I could ever regret what transpired between us. In truth, I want more. Much, much more. However, I am far too tired for that tonight.

That is why I merely smile up at him and place a soft kiss on his mouth. The taste of my blood makes me sigh.

"Take me to bed," I command.

Without delay, he does. Lifting me under my legs and against my back, he glides up the back stairs swiftly. I nod towards my back bedroom, and he enters the simple room. There is only a small wardrobe with my clothes, a simple four-poster bed with dark bedding, and a small side table. My sheets and pillows are still wrinkled from where I slept last night.

Setting me gently on my feet, I quickly toe off my boots and remove my dress before tossing it somewhere in the darkness. Now in only my shift, I fall forward into my bed before rolling onto my back. Through half-lidded eyes, I can see Eryx standing there. His face is unreadable in the dark light.

Too tired for words, I lift my hand and wave him forward. He hesitates for only a moment before following my order. Tentatively, he sits down on the bed, his posture awkward as he tries his best to squeeze into bed. He's kept his armor on, and his rigid posture doesn't look all that comfortable. Still, I don't have the energy to question it.

Reaching across the bed, I take his arm in mine and pull it towards me. Rotating to my side, I snuggle my body back against him. The metal places cool kisses against my heated skin. I settle against him with a sigh. We are still for a moment, and then I feel the quilt drape over us.

The last thing I remember before sleep claims me is the scent of metal and a sense of wholeness I haven't had since my mother passed.

I am no longer alone—and I never wish to be again.

6

NORY

The needle pricks my thumb, and I watch a droplet of red bloom on the tip.

With a gasp, I quickly suck the offending finger into my mouth. The metallic taste of my blood is tangy—different from how it was last night, from Eryx's lips. I silently curse myself for thinking of him again. He is the reason for my distraction this morning, which has led to no fewer than twelve different pricking incidents since I began mending the hem of this simple frock.

No matter how hard I try to put him out of my mind, my thoughts always wander back to him. A foolish thing to do, as clearly last night did not mean the same to him as it did to me. Waking alone in my bed, the indentation of his body beside me was the only evidence that the previous night had not been a dream.

Indeed, everything that had transpired was shockingly real. More confirmation that it had not been some fantasy came in the form of Isabelle, draped in her mourning dress. A black veil flowed down her back, but her eyes were shockingly clear. She had breezed in early this morning shortly after I had sat down to work.

The news of her husband's demise had come quickly after pleasantries.

"Dead—they found his body this morning. Killed by the same creature that had taken Lord Gunnar."

I willed my face to show a reasonable amount of shock; however, before I could form some sort of condolences, Isabelle had leaned down.

Her voice was barely above a whisper when she asked, "Did you have something to do with this, Nory?"

I reeled back, nearly tipping over my chair. My eyes shot to her children sitting thoughtfully on the porch, unaware of our hushed conversation.

"I—"

"The last anyone saw my husband, he was at Faulk's Tavern. A few patrons—along with Faulk himself—reported seeing him talking with a red-haired woman. However, it was too dark inside to get a good look at her. No one saw them leave together, but his body was found in the alley across the way." Isabelle licks her lips, eyes growing serious. "Nory, you knew of my plight. I had shared it with you that day, I just—"

Under her intense gaze, I said nothing—the silence was all the confirmation she seemingly needed to connect the puzzle pieces. A soft gasp escaped her lips before she nodded sharply. She had taken my hand in hers, her palm rough and warm.

"Thank you—thank you doesn't feel like enough," Isabelle whispered, but straightening up. "A monster killed my husband —that is all anyone will think, I'll make sure of it."

Reaching into her gown, she produced a large sack. Dropping it onto my work table, it rattled with the sound of hundreds of gold coins. My hands shook as I took it and peered at the wealth inside. I opened my mouth to protest, but Isabelle had silenced me with a hand.

"Good day, Nory. I wish you good health."

With that, she had turned in a flurry of black fabric, collected her children, and left my home, never looking back. I had stared at that sack of gold for a full hour. It was more than I had ever seen at one time in my life. I would have to mend over two hundred gowns to ever know that type of wealth again.

I had the good sense to hide the sack between a loose floorboard in the kitchen. I should've closed up shop; I had enough money to live off for a while. Yet, I found myself drawn back to my familiar routine. Isabelle's words replay in my mind.

A monster killed my husband—that is all anyone will think, I'll make sure of it.

A monster indeed, although after last night, he is more than that, isn't he? I sigh. My focus is once again back on him despite my best efforts. Leaning back in my chair, a familiar ache radiates up my spine. My sore muscles protest after being hunched over my work for so long. Rubbing my equally tired eyes reminds me just how taxing this craft is on my body.

If the younger me could see us now, she would be most displeased. That was back when I still dreamed of leaving the Snowlands—of making my way across the continent to a place free of frost and snow. To a place where the sea was crystal blue with white sand beaches instead of the brackish, ice-covered water and rough stone shores that make up our coastline. If such places exist, it would be just my luck to set out only to find everywhere is just as miserable as here.

I suppose I could ask Eryx; he's been alive for so long, surely he's seen what I seek.

Reflecting on those childish fantasies, I realize now what they had been a manifestation of—my fear. Not just of being stuck in the Snowlands, but of becoming my mother. The life of a seamstress is not an easy one, especially for a lone woman whose work was the only thing keeping her and her only child from the cold streets. I had watched each year take something from her.

Her brilliant auburn hair had gone completely white by the time she fell ill. When she passed, she looked far older than her forty-seven years—the decades of being bent over the work-table had permanently molded her spine in a soft curve. Her fingers—once slender and lithe—had frozen in odd angles with bumpy knuckles and calloused tips from the tedious work.

My heart aches for her as it always does. She was not given much of a choice. My father—may he rot wherever he is—was of no help. Mother rarely spoke of him. The few times she did was to tell me that he had been a traveler. They had fallen in love during the summer, and by the time the first frost came a month later, he was gone.

I was the only thing he had left behind.

There was a wistfulness in her gaze whenever she spoke about him. Like, somehow this was all some trick, and he would return, determined to be the husband and father we deserved. Though, as I grew older, it was clear he would not come back. Whatever fate befell him was more kind than he deserved.

While I am grateful for my existence, he saddled my mother with an insurmountable burden. Now that she's gone, I realize I am no better. Was it not my plan to abandon her as well? If only I could ask her—speak to her one last time—the illness had taken her mind long before it was through with her body.

There are questions I will never have answers to, and I'll have to make peace with that. Somehow.

A sharp bang, followed by a chorus of low bells, announces that someone has come through the front door. I glance up, my heart lifting for a moment, thinking it could be Eryx. What a strange turn of events that the creature I once ran screaming from, I now long to see more than all others.

Could he truly have disappeared? What of our bargain?

Those questions will have to wait as Eryx is not the one

who passes over my threshold. It is Kindell. I recognize her instantly. Her white blonde hair is pulled into a tight bun at the back of her head. We are the same age, even though it could be hard to tell. Her fine dress puts my casual one to shame. She has a baby swaddled across her chest and is clasping the palm of a girl no older than three in her other hand.

"Go sit over there. Quietly," she commands the older child, who dutifully does as she's told.

I rise from my work table and nod at her. Kindell had been a playful girl when we were young. The two of us would frolic through the farmers' land until sunset. Now, as I look into her tired eyes, she is little more than a wraith of the girl I once knew. Childrearing has taken a toll on her.

It's not surprising. Her father had been a strict man. Once Kindell was deemed old enough, he married her off to a nobleman, twice as wealthy as her father and more than twice Kindell's age.

"Hello, Nory." Kindell smiles, but it's tight, as if her muscles rarely perform the action. "It's been a long time."

"Indeed," I agree. "How can I help you? Do you need something fixed?"

I stare pointedly at her empty hands. If she had clothes for me, she hadn't seemed to bring them in. Kindell glances towards the door, as if to ensure it remains closed. With a loud swallow, Kindell steps closer, the edge of my table brushing the front of her gown.

"I—I've just come from Isabelle's. To offer my condolences for her husband's untimely passing." My stomach begins to sink, but I say nothing as she presses on. "She and I had formed a sort of bond these past few years. Our husbands both shared the same title...and vices..."

Kindell trails off, but I know full well what she means. Her husband, Lord Peter, has a reputation that rivaled Isabelle's for his debauched nature. Peter's cruelty was well-known. At least

Peter was more covert than Butch had been. Still, the signs of Kindell's misfortunes were apparent if you knew where to look.

"Please do not be angry with Isabelle," Kindell says in a rush. "She only told me as a means to help. I—I'm desperate, you see. Peter was always an awful man—from the moment we wed on the day of my eighteenth birthday, I have suffered under his hand."

Her palm lands atop the babe swaddled against her breast. Moisture collects in her eyes.

"After the birth of our second daughter, he became enraged." Kindell swallows thickly. "If the babe in my stomach now is not a boy, I fear how he will punish me and the girls."

I open my mouth but find no words to say. The tremble of her chin and the fear in her eyes makes my heart ache. I know before she even produces the sack of gold, I will help her. For who she was to me when we were girls, and because no one should have to suffer this way.

"He may be cruel, but a miser he is not," Kindell says, sliding the heavy sack of coins towards me.

The impeccable gown she wears indicates that Peter at least maintains appearances with his family. I reach for the bag and open it. My mouth dries at the sight. Hundreds of gold coins— jewels too—more than I received from Isabelle. With this wealth, I can stop working. I can do the things I dreamed of as a child. I can leave the Snowlands.

I shake myself before I get too lost in my fantasies. If I take her money, that means I have to make good on my promise to help her. I clasp the sack in my hands and meet her gaze.

"I will do what I can."

Kindell seems to sag with relief as she takes a few steps back from my table.

"Peter will be out this evening surveying some of the farm-land he's purchased that's been attacked by that creature. He takes the backroads home on horseback and will be alone."

I nod and watch as she quickly collects her other child and exits my home. Gazing out the front window, I watch her enter a fine carriage parked just outside my house before the driver signals the four proud horses into action.

With a groan, I collapse back into my chair. My back protests as I rub my sore eyes. Can I really do this again? Luring Butch from the tavern was one thing—this will require a bit more planning.

There is no time to waste. My red gown from the previous night will take some time to be washed and pressed for tonight. I have the means to help Kindell, and I will.

Right now, however, I have a demon to summon. One, I can only pray hasn't forgotten about his side of our bargain.

7

ERYX

The gnarled branches of the forest curl together overhead like finger bones.

The magic of *The Woods* dances on the mild wind, tugging at the ends of my frayed cloak. After wandering aimlessly, my destination finally appears in a small clearing. A decaying oak tree rests atop thick, bumpy roots and leaf litter. Its pale bark glows like the moon. Its leaves hang limply from twisting branches with dark sap bleeding from each frail stem.

The trunk is split in half, leaking more putrid sap down the front—magic pulses from the petrified tree. The metallic taste coats my tongue. It's been an age since I last found myself here in front of this deity.

God or goddess, I do not know. My maker has never been a creature of many words. Our paths had only crossed once before on the day I felt the oily lick of their magic during my creation. Since then, I have made it my mission never to go looking for my maker, lest they undo me on the spot. All of my kind that have ever gone searching for this power have met that fate.

Yet, foolishly, here I am standing in the shadow of their

great power for even the sliver of a chance to make things different. I'll beg if I have to—I'll do whatever I can for her.

Nory.

I'll beseech this deity for more time with her—to spend as much time with her as I am able. One night in her bed, holding her close, tasting her blood and her decadent mouth changed everything. I had made peace with my end as I had felt it looming for some time. In those dark, starving moments between feedings, I had longed for my undoing to stop this endless nothing.

Now I have a new lust for life brought about by my beautiful human. She is kind—brave—and so many other wonderful things. This cannot be the end of me, not when I've barely gotten a chance to explore her. I don't know how much time I have left, but it is not long. That is why I am here, begging this powerful being to be merciful.

Last night was a revelation. It had awoken something in me I didn't know I possessed. Feelings of longing and devotion followed me into sleep, where for the first time in centuries I dreamed. Glorious, warm dreams of Nory—of her face, her scent, of our life together, and what that could be. I never would've left her bed at the first rays of morning light if it hadn't been important. I had to find my maker and pay whatever price is necessary to stay my undoing.

With a sigh, I kneel on my cold armour plates before the imposing tree. They dig into my thin flesh, sending icy pricks along my body. Without Nory's warmth, I will surely freeze to death. Lowering my head and pressing my palms to my thighs, I assume a posture of pure supplication. The air around me goes still, the hum of life falls away.

A soft buzzing rattles my ears as my senses are overwhelmed with the scent of magic. The air thickens as the tree pulses before me. Dazzling white light spills from the broken trunk. It swirls around me—tendrils of power brush against my shoulders, and I suppress my shiver. After a few moments, the light consolidates into a solid form. My maker is made of only power, a being beyond this world that I am about to bargain with.

My plight is a foolish one, but for Nory, I would do anything to keep her at my side.

"My child," my maker hisses. "Coming before me now, when our eternal reunion is not too far off. Why?"

I swallow, tasting Nory's sweet blood faintly along my tongue.

"Dear maker—I've met someone. I come before you today as your humble servant, and beg you to postpone my undoing to give me more time with her."

The being glows brighter. The white light is too powerful for even my *lifefire* to stare at. The silence between us stretches, and unease tickles the back of my neck. Finally, my maker makes a soft chuffing sound. A laugh? Surely not. A being of this power has no use for fickle emotions such as humor.

"Does your human wish the same?"

My nod is emphatic. "Yes—yes, I believe so."

"Hmm," they hum. "Curious that. You are a monster—I made you that way."

"And I've felt like one for centuries. All until her. I beg of you, extend my time in this world at least until she reaches her own mortal end. A handful of decades—nothing more. I beseech you, dear maker."

Humans live such frightfully short lives. Merely blips in time compared to the centuries I've wandered. To think of Nory no longer being in this world makes my stomach hollow. Once she is gone, I will long for my undoing, knowing I could no longer roam this world without her in it.

My maker seems to consider my words, their stark light cooling in contemplation. After a moment, their rasping voice breaks the silence.

"Did you ever wonder why you were the last of your kind? My longest wandering creation that's outlived all the others."

"Stubbornness," I reply bitterly.

Again, a soft chuffing comes from them that I am forced to believe is the sound of amusement.

"My child, I made you different from the others. Many thought I was foolish to do so, seeing as you have not lived up to your full potential."

Their light fades nearly to gray.

"I apologize for displeasing you," I say. "Whatever it is you wish me to do, I will. So long as I can have more time with her."

"A lover's plight," they purr. "What's given must be earned, child. Never forget that."

Their light returns to brilliance as they float down from their perch atop the trunk. Self-preservation silences my tongue as I feel them float towards me. The whisper of warmth ghosts over my cold cheek, but I dare not look up.

"An extension will not be given on this day. In two weeks, you will be undone just like all the other revenants before you."

My stomach hollows as bile rises in my throat. The world tilts at odd angles around me. Two weeks is nothing. How will I ever—

"Unless," my maker sighs, "you do the one thing no one of your kind has done before."

Their power presses into the side of my face. I grit against the sting of their power cutting into the flesh of my cheek. Their light touches my ear, and in a hushed whisper, their demands are bestowed upon me. My lifeline from them is nothing more than an impossible ultimatum.

The last bit of my hope leaves me as they pull back.

"But how will I—"

"Silence. Those are my demands, and they must be met.

Speak to anyone about what I have told you, and my magic will undo you before your next breath."

Icy shock coats my skin in frost. Metal invades my lungs and coats my tongue. The light presses in on me, smothering me until there is no air left in my lungs. I choke, writhe on my knees before I feel the power snap. I greedily such down lungfuls of breath. A greasy sheen coats my skin, and I know our bargain is struck.

"Maker," I rasp, bowing my head.

By the time I gather the courage to look up, the being is gone. The clearing is just as still as I found it. I take stock of my body, feeling the familiar press of my armor and the worn edges of my cloak. One male entered this clearing, but another is leaving.

One who is determined to accomplish this daunting feat. I rise on shaking legs and turn back towards her—Nory. There is no time to waste. Each moment has become more precious than the last, with our finite time together barely more than a handful of days.

It spurs me to move fast—cutting through *The Woods* until I find myself at the outskirts of her town. Despite the odds, I have to try to fulfill this bargain.

Even if it kills me.

THIS PLAN she's presented me with has to be more foolish than the last.

I am pressed in amongst a clustering of evergreen trees, a few feet from the simple road. At least the scene before me looks believable enough. The only praise I can think of as I take in the broken horse's bridle in Nory's hand. We took it from the blacksmith's shop before making our way to a quieter part of the Snowlands.

The biting chill of the weather seemed worse out here for some reason. Yet, Nory was once again dressed in her scarlet dress. The way it hugged her body made my teeth grind together. Now that I know what she feels like against my palm, I have to swallow my groan and will my errant cock to behave.

Her pink cheeks and the loose tendrils of auburn hair clinging to her brow make her even more enticing. There is a tightness in her muscles, indicating her unease at the situation. Still, she is here to help—that kind heart of hers pounding soundly against her ribs. I can practically taste her pulse and hear the rushing of her sweet blood.

When I had returned from *The Woods*, it had been nearly late evening. I had snuck unseen into her cottage, finding her in a state. Was it merely my hope, or had she seemed genuinely pleased to see me? Like she had missed my presence throughout the day, and now that I had returned, she could relax. Her shoulders had sagged a bit upon my entrance. That has to mean something.

Unless it is my own unchecked fantasy, but then she said she believed I had departed early, forsaking our bargain entirely.

"I am a male of my word," I had said. "There is nothing in this world that could persuade me to leave with you on the line."

Color had stained her round cheeks, and the look of plea-sure danced in her green eyes. The subject of my abandonment was dropped then, and she imparted to me her ludicrous plan.

Her soft heart had been on full display as she told me about the woman she longed to help. Nory is unlike any human I have ever met. Her kindness is uncommon. However, the more I think about it, the more I realize that might not be true. Maybe I have just spent too much time on my own—wrestling with my own misery—that I never took the chance to learn about another human.

To be fair, none of them who saw me for more than a moment seemed inclined to hold a polite conversation. Nory is different in that regard—she summoned me, boldly and unafraid. Still, I am far from angry when I consider Nory being the first and last human I'll ever truly know.

Each moment with her is a gift—and that is why I have no plans to tell her of our limited time together. Suppose there is any chance of making good on this bargain imposed on me by my maker, then I could not tell her. If she learned of my predicament, it may taint what was between us. The burden is mine and mine alone. More so, I would not want her to submit to me out of pity.

That would be a fate worse than death.

I will endure in silence and be grateful for the moments we share in whatever capacity they may come. Watching her petite frame shiver, I know it's not merely from the cold but from what we are about to do. She should have no part in this. If she simply gave me a name, I could dispatch these men for her.

Nory hadn't gone for that idea, telling me she had to do it. That, even if it was a small part, she had to know she helped in some way. Her words float back to me from the night before. She enjoys my power—how I will kill for her at the slightest provocation. It is at odds with her good nature, but then perhaps not entirely. The Snowlands are a harsh place for anyone to grow up in. There is a darkness that infects all who live here. Nory's darkness has just manifested in this way, and I am more than happy to be the outlet for her wicked ways.

Is that not proof that she is perfect for me in all ways? She is the one thing I've spent centuries looking for: her heart, her soul, her beauty, all of it mine. I just need a chance to prove myself worthy of her devotion. If I do, then maybe she will—

The soft clicking of hooves on stone steals my attention.

I tuck myself firmly into the dark treeline, hidden in shadow. Tilting my head around the nearest tree, I can make out the lone rider who approaches the magnificent, glittering brown steed. He is an older man, with gray at his temples and lines around his eyes and mouth. The state of his clothing is impeccable. His coat is trimmed in fine gold thread and adorned with matching buttons. Broad of shoulder and long of leg, he must be nearly twice as old as Nory.

I glance over to her and watch her morph into the perfect distraction: a distressed damsel whose horse has bolted and left her stranded along the road.

She waves a delicate hand and smiles warmly at the approaching man.

The man stops—of course he does—and seals his fate.

"Trouble?" The buttons of his coat refract the moonlight as he hitches his horse to a nearby post.

"L–Lord Peter," Nory whispers, throwing back her shoulders and exposing more creamy skin. "My horse. I—I don't know what happened. An owl must've scared it—the poor darling snapped free and took off before I barely got my bearings about me."

Through narrowed eyes, I watch the man—Lord Peter—survey the scene for any hints of deception. Nory withers his inspection, and I see the moment his gaze turns from weary to lecherous. My teeth grind together as he stares pointedly at the swells of her breasts. My fingers sink into the bark of the nearest tree, coating my hands in wood shavings.

I can practically hear his horrid thoughts. He's thanking his good fortune for coming across such a sight. A lone woman—beautiful and alluring—in need of help along a secluded road. In his haste to have her, he will not realize that a monster lurks in her shadow, ready to strike. She commands me to kill, and I am all too happy to oblige.

The hunger inside me roars, needing to spill his blood this instant. Still, I wait for her signal—ever the humble servant.

"I'm sorry," Nory says, tears pooling in her eyes. Ever the convincing actress. "It's just I'm all alone and I don't know—"

"Hush," Peter purrs. "You are safe now. I'll escort you back to town."

Nory swipes at her eyes with the sleeve of her scarlet gown. Her cloak has fallen entirely off her shoulders, and the gown molds to each supple curve. Lord Peter takes notice, as do I. Nory smiles at the man, but there is an edge to it that the other man is all too happy to ignore.

"Really?"

"Of course." His eyes turn heated as his hand raises to touch her cheek. "My, what a beautiful young woman you've turned into. I remember when you and my wife were just girls."

Anger flashes in her verdant gaze, but she remains composed. I want to flay him alive for daring to touch her soft skin. She is mine—the only hands to touch her will be mine.

"T—thank you, sir."

With a sigh, Lord Peter's hand drifts lower and locks around her upper arm. Nory's eyes go wide at the touch, and she gently tries to pull back.

"Lord Peter?"

"Hush now, my sweet. Now, don't you want to show me a little gratitude for my help?"

"I—no. Stop!"

Nory shoves against his hold. Her small hands connect with his chest, but it is of no use. His other hand wraps around her back, pinning her to him.

"Be quiet!" he hisses. "Don't make a sound while—"

I can stomach no more and launch myself from the treeline. The frosty grass crunches under my feet, but neither one of them notices I've moved until I am upon them. With a roar, I rip the man from Nory. He cannot get a word out before I have him pinned to a nearby tree. His eyes are wild, and I let my *lifefire* roar into an inferno. The flames bathe his face in harsh shadows.

"I—I—"

The man blubbers in my grip, the scent of urine covering up the potent smell of his fear. My eyes go to Nory, who stands nearby. Her eyes are wide—not in fear but in excitement. Her gaze locks with mine, and she nods.

"Do it."

I snarl, pushing his head back. My lips find his ear.

"You will die here. The birds will feed on your corpse, and you will become nothing." Lord Peter fights me, but it is of no use. "No one will remember you."

Lord Peter jolts towards me, and there is an odd pressure in my stomach. Pulling back from him slightly, I glimpse the polished handle of a dagger now protruding from my abdomen. Nory gasps as I wrap a hand around the blood and pull. Dark blood coats the sharp end.

I chuckle darkly before tossing it into the ground beside me.

"Foolish mortal," I hiss. "I cannot be killed. Not like that."

The other man's eyes go wide with fear—his final expression as I sink my teeth into the fleshy skin of his neck. I drink down his putrid blood. His vile soul has tainted it, and compared to Nory's, it nearly makes me gag. Still, I drink and drink until he goes cold in my arms. Once I've had my fill, I drop him.

His body hits the ground with a thud—his eyes open towards the moon, but he sees nothing.

Turning from his body, I nearly tumble into Nory. She's close—almost as close as she was to me the previous night. Her eyes are wide with worry, not for Lord Peter but for me as she gently touches my wound. My hand comes down atop hers, and she shivers.

"Are you alright?" she asks, eyes staring up at me in wonder.

"Fine. Already healed." I press her hand to the closed skin in confirmation.

Nory sighs, her shoulders sagging.

"I didn't know he was armed. I didn't—"

She breaks off in a violent shiver. Color suddenly leeches from her face. My hand rises to her cheek, forcing her eyes to remain on me. Her hands fall to my arms as if to keep her upright.

"Are you alright?"

"Yes," she whispers, licking her lips. "I'm glad he's dead. Kindell will be free from him—he was a cruel man."

I nod, not knowing what else to say. Some of Nory's coloring returns as she shakes herself. With one last squeeze to my arms, she takes a step back, and I immediately want to reach for her again.

"We should head back," I offer.

Nory stomps over to Lord Peter's horse and unties it from the post. With a sound smack on the animal's rump, it goes galloping off down the road. We both watch it disappear into the horizon for a moment before Nory turns towards me.

"Once the horse returns without him, Lord Peter's staff will send out a search party," Nory explains. "We should cut through *The Woods* to remain unseen."

Without another word, I take her small hand in mine and lead her towards the dark forest. My vision in the dark is much better than hers without the moon to illuminate a path. I dutifully maneuver us over tree roots and fallen branches. All is quiet as we pass through the dense foliage. Our journey is short as I spy the graveyard up ahead.

It is only when we pass by the first few headstones that I feel Nory's hand fall from mine.

I whirl towards her. Her eyes are like I've never seen before, burning brighter than emeralds. There is a determined set to her brows, and her hands are steady as they lift to the tie of her cloak. With one tug, the cloak falls from her shoulders and lands at her feet in a brown heap.

"Nory?"

She bites her lip, walking closer to me.

"Are you hungry?" Her voice is pure seduction.

The swells of her breast tease the low neckline of her scarlet gown. With so much smooth, supple flesh on display, my mouth begins to water.

"Yes," I groan.

Nory's pink lips curve in satisfaction. I watch entranced as her hands fall to the back of her gown. With a few expert tugs, the red gown gapes at the top, then drops to her feet. She kicks it away, and I hear my breath echoing in my ears. Her pale arms glow in the moonlight. Freckles decorate every inch of exposed skin, and I long to taste and count each one of them.

To see if they are near her most intimate flesh.

"What are you doing?" My voice sounds foreign to my own ears.

Her eyes burn brighter, but she merely smirks as she undoes the laces of her corset. It soon rests atop her gown, leaving her in nothing but a thin shift. I can make out the shape of her body. Two hard nipples press against the fabric, making my head spin.

"I don't want to wait until we get home," she sighs.

Before I can ask what she means, her hands fall to the straps of her shift and pluck them from her shoulder. The white cotton floats like a cloud and falls to the frozen ground. My whole body tightens at the sight of her completely bare.

Creamy skin decorated in a smattering of golden freckles is all I can see. Her small breasts are tipped in pink nipples, and between her thighs. *Dear maker*, there is a nest of dark hair covering the most delicious-looking flesh. Her scent of arousal invades my lungs and encourages my cock to harden further.

It presses against the front of my pants, already leaking seed and desperate to be attended to in any way. This painful state is new and belongs to Nory. She will be the only one to determine if I writhe in agony or am I treated to the bliss of pleasure.

Stepping over her clothes, she walks towards me dressed in only her boots.

"Nory—"

Before I can say anything more, she takes my hand and places it on her breast. The heat of her skin burns my palm.

"Touch me," she whimpers. "Where no man has ever before."

My grip on her tightens. I want to devour her whole, but I somehow manage to hold myself back. I wait for her to come to her senses—for the desire in her gaze to clear. It doesn't.

She merely tips her face towards mine, and my lips find hers in one bruising, burning kiss.

8

NORY

The biting night wind is forgotten the moment his lips touch mine.

I am nothing but sensation and aching need as his mouth devours mine. Our kiss is frantic as if making up for lost time—then it turns slower, a silken glide of our tongues tangling together. His hands rasp over my bare skin, making me shiver. Leaning into his body, warmth like I've never felt before envelopes me.

One slender hand travels up my ribs to cup my breasts. Curious fingers tug at my nipples until I'm gasping into his mouth. He swallows the sound, and I push myself further against him—feeling his aching hardness against my stomach.

It had been a spur-of-the-moment decision to take this risk with him. One that my head had been firmly against. However, now that I feel him against me, I'm glad I threw caution to the wind. While I may not entirely know this male—this creature —what I do know is I've never felt fear like that when I saw Peter's dagger protruding from his stomach.

When he returned to my home earlier this afternoon, something had shifted between us. If I'm honest with myself, it's clear that I missed him and the thought of never seeing him again...

My stomach hollows, and I grip him tighter. It made me realize that he's the only other being ever to make me feel like this. Safe—protected at all costs—and inflames my desire to the point where I'm desperate with need.

This potent lust spurned me to shed my clothes and let him have me before my brain could think of reasons not to. I don't want to wait—I don't want any more of my life to pass me by without claiming what I want.

I want him. Eryx. More than anything, I want his mouth and hands on me. I want to feel him moving within me—stoking this fire inside of me until I combust. Our time together is limited. I can feel it with each starving kiss we share. It won't be long before the townsfolk come hunting for answers. We'll slip up. Kindell or Isabelle will gossip to the wrong person, and that will be the end of me.

Or something else will separate us—something I can't see but can feel lurking in the shadows. Our time together is finite. The desperation in the way he touches me is confirmation enough that we both feel it. I do not know how much time we have, only that anything less than forever will not be enough. That is why I couldn't delay a moment longer. I had to have him.

Now.

For so long, I believed something was wrong with me. Unlike the other women my age, I never felt a sense of longing or desire for any of the men in the Snowlands—not even for the handsome travelers that would pass through. I was resigned to spending my life alone, especially after my mother passed. I made peace with it, even if my heart ached over never knowing the intimacy that blossomed on the page of my weathered romance novels and love poems.

But I feel that wanton desire now—for Eryx, a revenant of

all things. He is much more than that to me now. He is my protector—my savior—but gratitude is not what made me drop my dress. It was him, and I intend to make him mine before the sun rises.

His hand on my breasts tightens before he pulls away from my mouth. Whimpering in protest, my hands fall to his back, desperate to pull him closer. The fire in his eyes glows blue.

"Are you certain you want this?" he asks, voice rougher than stone.

"More than anything," I sigh, reaching up to capture his mouth again.

I moan as he returns my kiss, unsure of just when I became such a vixen. I revel in his touch and encourage his gentle exploration with soft moans. His fingers splay over my back and coast down my spine. Goosebumps rise in their wake as our tongues dance together. Fingers sink into the fleshy swell of my ass, and I groan. My thighs rub together, moisture blooming between them.

Eryx's forehead rests against mine, his hands gently squeezing my ass.

"You're so beautiful," he growls, the vibrations of his chest tickling my nipples. "The males of your kind were never worthy enough to have you."

"You are though. More than worthy." I rub against his stiff cock and delight in his hiss of breath. "Take me."

Kissing along my jaw, Eryx chuckles darkly against my skin. I shiver when his lips lick a path of fire to my ear.

"I've never had a female before."

Satisfaction flows through my veins and warms my heart. My well of pleasure deepens at the idea of being the first and only to claim him—for us to claim each other.

"Nor have I been with a man." My hand skims over his cheek. "We'll navigate this together."

Eryx nods into my palm. Tenderness kindles in his eyes. He

kisses me soundly again, and I indulge in his taste—crisp like midnight air. Breaking our kiss with the wave of his hand, I watch as my discarded clothes float on a breeze before being laid out by invisible hands atop the sparse grass. Eryx's hands return to my hips, digging into my bones there before hefting me gently in his grasp.

In one fluid motion, he lays me atop my clothes. The moonlight bathes my naked skin in blue. Each freckle stands out starkly against my pale skin. There is a flush to my chest and knees that deepens as I stare up at Eryx.

He looks every bit the monster looming over me. His dark cloak sprawls out behind him like a shadow. The flames of his eyes have turned a fiery blue, and the hue of his waxy skin begins to glisten. Metal floats through the air, nearly blighting his woodsy scent.

My knees inch together under his stare, and he growls. Falling to his knees before me, his armor clanks on the dark ground. His hands cup my knees as he gently peels them apart, revealing my most intimate flesh to another's eyes for the first time. Heat sprawls up my chest and burns my cheeks as I watch the hunger in his gaze deepen—moisture slicks from between my folds in a steady rivulet.

I have no doubt the fabric beneath me is sodden with my arousal.

Eryx falls forward onto me. His hard body is cushioned by my much softer one. His lips find mine as his hands spear into my hair, anchoring me to him. My thighs open in a sweet burn to accommodate the stretch of him. Is this how it will feel once he is inside of me?

His mouth travels lower, nipping at my jaw before licking into the hollow of my throat. I moan, rubbing my nipples against the rigid plates of his armor. He tastes me fully—savoring every inch of my skin. I gasp as his mouth kisses between my breasts. Eryx smiles against me, and we lock eyes as he takes one of my nipples into his mouth. A moan falls from my lips. My back arches off the ground as he sucks the tight peak deep into his mouth.

Eryx's other hand rises to tease my other nipple. Over and over, he works my breast with his tongue, alternating between hard licks and gentle nips. Switching his attention to my other breast, my eyes flutter close. Lifting my hips, my aching core flexes around nothing—desperate to be filled. I rub it against him, hoping to find any relief.

He leaves my breast with a pop and gently kisses down my stomach. Once he is at the cradle of my hips, he cups both my knees and gently pushes them even farther apart. Inhaling deeply, he throws me a wicked grin as he stares down at my wet flesh.

"I killed for this little wet pussy," he snarls. "I'd do it a thousand times to have you spread out before me like this. A feast to enjoy at my leisure."

Words escape me. All I can do is nod frantically as he stares at my feminine flesh. Inhaling deeply once more, I watch him lower his face between my thighs. Another deep inhale makes him shudder, then pull back. My eyes fly open as I whimper. Thrusting my lower half towards him, Eryx gazes down at me, chest rising and falling with quick breaths.

Fingers inch closer to my opening but quickly retreat. A frustrated growl leaves my lips, earning me a chuckle from Eryx.

"Desperate thing you are," he sighs. "Beg."

I gasp at the fire in his gaze, swirling to deep red. My pussy clamps around nothing, making me even more desperate than before.

"What?" I ask.

"Beg me to lick this sweet pussy. Make it convincing, and I might indulge you."

My desperation makes me indignant, and I raise a brow.

"For someone who's never been with a woman, you are quite confident in your skills. How can I be certain they are worth begging for?"

A wicked grin curves his lips.

"You'll be the only one ever to call my bluff." His fingers trail down my inner thighs. "Something tells me I'll have no problem satisfying you."

I bite my lip. I've never asked a male for anything—let alone begged one. However, Eryx isn't just any male. He makes me feel safe—safe enough to shed the hard exterior I've had to craft to survive in the Snowlands. With him, I can be me and let this desire unfurl inside of me.

My submission comes easily enough, the icy walls of my trepidation melting under his stare.

"Please," I whimper. "Please, Eryx. Lick me. I need it—I'm so desperate for you, I'm going out of my mind."

My cheeks burn as do my eyes. The denial of my pleasure is making me crazed with lust.

"Taste my pussy. Claim it—it was always yours. Please. I need you."

"And what do you need from me?"

"Your tongue." I swallow thickly. "And your cock."

Eryx chuckles darkly, his hands sliding up to grip my hips.

"Good girl," he praises. "You shall have both tonight."

Without warning, he scoops my bottom half clean off the ground. My legs fall over his shoulders as the cold metal of his armor presses into my flesh. A scream of pleasure is ripped from my lips at the first glide of his tongue up my slit. The sensation is far too intense to be explained. My hands grip the dress below me, and I dig my heels into his shoulders.

His lick is gentle—exploring—and is quickly followed by another. Then another. My eyes turn heavy at each pass of his tongue. The sensation is heavenly. Pleasure coils deep in my stomach.

Eryx growls against me as he devours. His tongue parts me and tickles my clit. I moan deeply at the new onslaught of pleasure. He alternates between tasting and sucking the pleasurable spot. My revenant is not practiced in his movements. Instead, he listens to my body's responses. Trying out new ways to pleasure me and gauging my reaction.

When his tongue pushes into my entrance, I nearly lose my mind. It is a tentative taste at first as he parts me. My arousal and his wet tongue aid him in gliding deeper into me before pulling back. Again, he swirls that silk muscle inside of me, wiggling it just right.

"Eryx," I moan, wriggling his grasp. "Please."

His eyes burn bright, and his fingers press into my backside to hold me firm to his face. His tongue enters me again, stretching deep. My vision turns blurry as he continues to push inside of me. The burn is sweet, but I know it'll be nothing compared to his cock. His tongue continues to stretch deep into me—farther than any tongue should. Wetness pools from my opening as his tongue retreats before thrusting back in.

Over and over, he fucks me with his tongue until my teeth clench together. On an intense thrust, his tongue brushes a hidden spot inside of me. He groans as he tickles it, and my body grows tight with pleasure. Every muscle in my body is primed—ready to explode.

The wet, sloppy sounds of my pussy echo around us in the graveyard. The night is still. The only witness to our coupling is the moon glowing above. One hand leaves my ass to work circles on my clit. My hips canter at the touch, my moans becoming desperate.

His tongue slips from me as he savors my taste.

"So sweet," he groans. "Your virgin pussy is desperate for my claim. For a monster who feeds on the dead. How fitting it is that a graveyard is the first place I'll take you."

His words spur me on, pleasure wraps around me. His

tongue enters me again—thick and seeking—while his fingers play with my clit. That's all it takes before my climax consumes me. Fire licks up my skin as I scream his name up at the night sky. My pussy locks around his tongue, and he fucks me through it. Tasting and biting until the shudders lessen.

Trembling, Eryx settles me back to the ground before prowling up my body again. His lips find mine, and he shares the salty taste of my arousal. Even though my muscles feel like jelly, I begin turning slippery between my thighs again—eager for more. His eyes are tender as he smooths hair from my sweaty brow.

Locking my legs around his hips, I nip at his chin.

"Take me, Eryx." Lifting my chin, I present him my throat. "Bite me while you do it."

He hisses before nodding. Reaching up, I untie his cloak and toss it somewhere in the dark. I fumble between our bodies, finding the top of his pants, and I push them down. My mouth dries at the first glimpse of him.

Waxy skin covers his long, thick shaft. The tip is a pale gray, already leaking a pearl of sticky seed. Along the sides are not veins but raised ridges that come to dull points. I shiver at the thought of them gliding along my inner walls. Eryx is obscenely large, and I wonder how he's going to fit inside of me.

"Don't worry, Nory. Your pretty pussy is wet enough. I'll fit nice and snug inside that tight hole of yours."

I nod, my whole body trembling. His thumb slicks over his tip, using the bead of wetness to coat his cock. My legs fall to the side as he lines himself up with my entrance. My heart pounds in my chest, and my breathing shudders out of me. Eryx sucks in a breath as he tucks himself into my entrance.

In one slow thrust, he enters me. Pushing with controlled speed until he's fully seated inside of me. The barrier preventing his invasion has been done away with. There is only the sweet sting of him stretching me and his pulsing cock. It's so warm I feel as though I'm being filled with fire. The ridges scrape along my inner walls, making my head spin.

His hands plant firmly on either side of my face. Eryx's body trembles, trying his best not to move while I adjust to him. Our breathing is ragged. The sensation of him inside of me snaps any lingering restraint. I am his and he is mine. There is nothing between us now but pleasure. I want to lose myself in him.

"Eryx," I whimper, lifting my hips. "Fuck me. Please."

"Fuck," Eryx hisses, retreating and then pushing back into me.

Moans slip from between my lips as he thrusts into me again. The feeling of him inside me already has my body racing towards another peak.

"Tightest little pussy. All mine."

"Yours," I agree.

Eryx snarls, retreating until only the tip of his cock remains in me before thrusting deep. My breasts bounce as pleasure steals my breath.

"Look at how greedy you are for my cock. If only those vile men could see you, knowing a monster is ravaging you. I should've fucked you in front of them before killing them. That way they'd die knowing who you've always belonged to."

His hands hook around my hips as he fucks me onto his length. His ridges tickle that spot deep inside of me. His crude words enhance my pleasure. I want his claim on me—I need it. He is the only being I'll belong to. I saved myself for him, and he did the same for me.

"Your little cunt is tightening on me, Nory. Do you like the idea of that—of me laying claim to you?"

"I—I—"

"I have half a mind to drag you into the center of town. For your screams of pleasure to wake your neighbors from their beds. And when they come to explore the noise to find you like this. Begging for my cock."

"Yes. Yes!" I whimper, my peak looming closer. "Fuck me in front of them. However you want—wherever. I'm yours."

"Mine," Eryx growls.

His lips find mine in a bruising kiss. Each thrust wrecks my body and heats my blood. His tongue tangles with mine as he devours my moans. My hands fall to his shoulders and pull him closer. Eryx leaves my mouth and pulls back. My arms float to my sides as he stares down at me. The fire in his gaze blazes as he withdraws from me.

Immediately, I feel the loss of our connection, and I reach for him. He doesn't leave me for long. Sliding beside me, he angles my body onto its side. I watch as he lifts my leg and lines up his cock with my entrance from behind. With a thrust, he's back inside of me. Bliss wraps around my body as I sigh.

The fit is much tighter this way. His cock reaches deeper into me.

"My beautiful, perfect Nory," he purrs in my ear. "I am a male of my word, as you know."

I gasp as his hand raises to play with my nipples. His tongue licks along my throat, and I shiver in anticipation. Behind me, his thrusts become more frantic. Each one steals my breath with its power. His hips bounce off my ass as my climax draws closer.

I can't catch my breath. He is all I smell—all I feel. There is no way to tell where he begins and where I end. We are one. Now. Forever. The thought steals my breath, but I mean it. From this day forward, I never want to be parted from him.

With a groan, his teeth embed themselves in the side of my neck. I hear him suck at my flesh, and my whole body erupts. Euphoria unleashes inside of me, and my body is awash in fire. Pleasure tightens every muscle. I clench down on his thrusting cocking. Eryx tightens his hold on me fucking me through my climax until I finally come down.

Once I am merely a mess of quivering muscles, Eryx releases my neck. I shiver as he licks at my wound before nuzzling into me. He places lazy kisses atop my temple and cheeks. The world around me barely registers. However, there is one thing that is rousing me to awareness.

"You—you did not—"

"Come?" Eryx supplies, and I nod.

Kissing my lips, he withdraws from me.

"Your blood is all that I need."

Before he can roll away from me, I grab his arm. His eyes blaze as I push him onto his back. Slinging my leg across his hip, I ignore the soreness of my muscles and place both my hands atop his cold armor. My pussy glides along his cock, still hard and leaking seed.

"Would you deny me your seed?" I ask. "Have I not earned it?"

My face twists into a pout as I bite my lip. Eryx groans as his hands fall to my hips. Gently, I rock atop his cock, coating it in my wetness.

"Be sure of what you ask, Nory. If I finished inside you I'd—"

"What?" I ask.

Stopping my movements, I grip him in my hand, gently stroking him. Waxy skin glides against my palm, and my mouth waters. I want to taste him, but not yet. I want to feel him spill deep inside of me. I'll get my lips around him another time.

His fingers press into my hips.

"I'd have to fuck you every day. Spill my seed inside you— coat you in it. Mark you inside and out."

I shiver at his words. Lifting on my knees, I wriggle around atop his cock until I fit him perfectly at my entrance.

"Good," I say, before sinking down on him.

He is sheathed inside me with a throaty moan. My ass rests atop his thighs, the cold armor cutting into my skin. Raising myself again, I lower back down, taking him even deeper. I'll be sore tomorrow, but it is more than worth it watching Eryx come undone below me. His hands grip my hip before one travels to my bouncing breast.

I work myself up and down his length as his eyes swirl with fire. He urges me to move fast, his mouth open as a torrent of groans spills from it. The wet smack of bodies echoes around us. If anyone happened upon us, I can only imagine they'd go running from the obscene sight.

However, just like when Eryx mentioned fucking me in front of the whole town, the idea makes me wild with desire. It is wrong, but I can't help but revel in it. Perhaps I've always been a little wicked, and it just took a monster to awaken it in me.

Being with Eryx has made me bolder—more confident. I fuck him faster and faster. My climax looms once more as I manage to rub my clit against him. Eryx lifts his hips, deepening each thrust. My movements become halting, pleasure stealing my strength.

Wrapping his arms around me, Eryx holds me aloft as he powers into me from below. After a particular hard thrust, I erupt. My pussy locks around his cock like a vise, and Eryx bellows before filling me with a rush of his hot seed. Warm, sticky spend spills deep inside me before overflowing and sliding down my thighs. My heart hammers against my ribs, and pleasure steals my words.

Eryx fucks into me once, twice more, ensuring I've taken all of his seed. Once we are both coming down, he rolls us onto our sides. His arms cocoon me into his warmth. We stare up at each other, sharing ragged breaths.

We don't speak. We don't have to, for it's written plainly on both of our faces. Everything has changed here in this grave-yard. Surrounded by death, I've never felt so alive.

My life belongs to him. No matter how much time we have together, I will fight for every moment. I will fight to keep him. For now, tiredness is seeping into my bones, and my eyes grow heavy.

Snaking my leg around his hip, I burrow into his chest.

"Take my home," I whisper against his skin.

Eryx's laugh is the sweetest sound.

"Always."

9

NORY

Golden sunlight streams into my eyes, rousing me from a deep slumber.

Blinking against the offending light, I take in my familiar room. Everything is just as I left it the night before. My worn boots are resting against the wall while my cloak hangs from the lone peg beside the door. The wrinkled fabric of my scarlet gown lies in a pool at the foot of my bed. Fresh laundry remains in folded stacks that I have yet to put away.

The only unusual thing in this room is the male body spooned around me.

His soft skin rests me. The weight of his arm along my side and his soft breaths against my shoulder send a delicious shiver through me. Eryx had removed his cloak and armor last night as we shared a warm bath to wash away the night's chill. The sight of his tall form, adorned with lean muscles, had stolen my breath.

There was nothing about him that was human. Dark blood flowed in his gray veins. He was not human—but neither was he a monster. At least he wasn't to me. His primal nature and formidable form excite me. I desire him above all else.

Watching the bath water lap at his pale skin had ignited another inferno of lust inside of me.

It led me to seek him out and join our bodies together once more. We had come at the same moment amongst the cooling water before he lifted my trembling body from the tub. Depositing us both on the bed, he gathered me to him before we both fell asleep.

After our teeth-clenching rounds of lovemaking, it seems my revevant needs his sleep. His eyes remain closed—his pale lips are parted slightly as he dreams. In the silence of the morning, I take him in, careful not to move and rouse him. Sunlight dances across the sharp angles of his face, making his pale skin glow. He doesn't seem so foreboding in sleep. Instead, all I can see is Eryx...the male I care for.

That feels too simple a word to describe my feelings towards Eryx. After last night, things have changed between us. I can still feel him inside me. The phantom imprint of his body lingers along my skin. The threads of our souls weave together in a new, permanent pattern that cannot be undone. Most shockingly of all, I no longer feel alone.

Eryx is with me now, and I know we will never be parted.

Even as I think it, uneasiness rises within me like a wave. These feelings he's stirred inside me are dangerous—making me uncertain of the future for the first time in years. Despite my heart's urging to yield to him completely, I can't shake this feeling that our time together is rapidly dwindling. The thought of not having him causes my heart to pound.

How has he managed to become so integral to me in such a short amount of time?

You would be fine if he left, a traitorous voice whispers. *Life would be simple again, and you'd have enough money to do as you please. Alone.*

I shake myself to silence that errant voice. These warring

feelings have left me off-kilter. I don't have to make any decisions—at least not right now. I hope that is.

A soft clicking sound makes my eyes snag at the clock on the wall. The hands read well past eight in the morning. With a deep sigh, I stretch my arms above my head. Customers will be arriving soon to collect their garments. No doubt Kindell will return to give thanks for her husband's demise—surely he's been found by now. It's likely to be quite the gossip today, and I'll have to feign my ignorance of the whole ordeal.

The stirring beside makes me turn in his grasp. Eryx's eyes blink open, and pale yellow light glows from within his sockets. A lazy grin curves his lips as his hand tightens along my bare hip.

"Good morning," he purrs in his deep voice.

"Morning." Warmth envelopes my cheeks as I feel his cock harden against me. "My customers will be arriving in an hour to collect their orders."

Eryx nods, but makes no move to release me. He does the opposite, dragging me into his chest. The quilt slips from my shoulders and bares my breasts to his hungry gaze. Eryx's thin fingers cup my breasts before gently rubbing my nipples, encouraging them into stiff peaks. I moan at the touch as my body begins to heat.

"The world seeks to take you away from me this morning," he murmurs. "How are you feeling?"

I force my heavy-lidded eyes open as he continues to work me.

"Perfect. More than perfect."

"Happy?" he asks. I hear the unease in his voice.

Meeting his gaze with my own, I cup his cheek, laying bare the desire for him in my eyes, and I nod. There is no room for uncertainty between us. I watch as his body relaxes and leans down to capture my nipple in his mouth. Moaning against him, I cradle his head to me, urging him to taste me more.

After a few devastating licks of his tongue, he releases my nipple with a pop. Arousal spreads down my inner thighs, desperate for relief. Eryx inhales deeply, a wicked smile on his mouth.

"In all the damned centuries I've prowled this world, I've never felt like this before. Blood fulfilled me—it was the only thing I ever craved—but now I could live off your taste alone. Until the world around us crumbles into dust." Flames roar to life in his eyes. "You are a madness—burrowing under my skin and into my dead heart."

The organ remains still, never pounding in the same rhythm mine does. With a growl, his lips capture mine in a searing kiss. Pushing me back onto the mused sheets, he falls between my spread thighs. I moan as his mouth leaves me to kiss a trail of fire down my throat. My hips lift to rub my wetness along his hard cock. The ridges tease my clit and make more arousal leak from me.

"You are my madness, too." My breathy confession comes as he latches onto my breast again. "With you, I can be who I truly am."

His mouth leaves my breath to kiss down my stomach. Eryx's wet tongue dips into my navel, and my breathing turns into ragged pants as he kisses across my hip bones.

"All it took was spilling some blood for you to assure you of my devotion. With me, you'll always be protected—guarded like the treasure you are," he growls against my trembling skin. "I'll slaughter every male in this town if you will it—anything to get my cock back into this tight pussy of yours."

Rising up, he takes his cock into his hand. A shimmering drop of wetness beads at the tip as he lines it up with my entrance. Rubbing himself between my folds, my eyes blur at the sensation. I open my mouth to tell him to take me—to claim me in the light as thoroughly as he did in the dark.

Before I can, there's a sharp knock at the door. My pleasure shatters like a dropped glass. Eryx holds himself still atop me, head whipping towards the sound. Beyond my pounding heart beat, I can just make out a sound coming from beyond the door —voices—a handful of them overlapping in hushed conversation.

This can't be good.

Ice coats my veins as my mind immediately drifts to the worst outcome. My plots have been uncovered, and the men of this town have come to take me away to pay for my crimes. Rational finally creeps in as I realize they would've broken down the door right by now to haul me off.

Still, I have no appointments this early—whoever is at my door is not here to see a seamstress.

The bed creaks as Eryx rolls off of me and onto the floor. His eyes blaze towards the front room.

"Stay here. I'll deal with whoever's out there."

While I appreciate the sentiment, I'm not in the mood to clean blood off my porch. Besides, this could have a reasonable explanation, and I don't want him in danger over something I can quickly dispel on my own. Rising from the bed, I catch my breath at the soreness between my legs. I don't have time to register the stiffness as I reach out and snag Eryx's arm.

"Let me handle it," I say, shaking my head when he opens his mouth to argue. "Stay hidden back here. Hopefully it won't come to this, but if things do take a turn—"

"I won't hesitate to protect you."

"I know."

Pushing up on my toes, I capture his lips. No longer being alone has made me bolder. Whatever waits on that other side of the door will not harm me—Eryx will keep me safe. He deepens our kiss. Our tongues glide together, but before we can get carried away, another barrage of knocks echoes through the house. I sigh, pulling back. Eryx's gaze is still wary as he glares towards the door.

"I'll be fine."

At least, I hope I will.

Quickly, I rifle through my clean clothes and find a simple cotton dress. The green material is thick enough that I forgo a corset and stuff my feet into a pair of soft slippers. Braiding my hair back, I secure it with a ribbon. Staring into the mirror, I'm shocked at the face I see staring back. She doesn't look like me —her green eyes glow brightly, and there is a permanent flush to her cheeks.

I shake myself and turn away from my appearance. With one more nod towards Eryx, I watch him slink into the shadows of my room. Hustling through the house, I side-step stacks of repaired hems and pants until my hand wraps around the old brass knob. Taking a deep breath, I twist the handle and meet what awaits me on the side.

Gathered on my stoop is a group of ten women—Kindell leads them at the front, dressed in her mourning weeds. Her eyes are clear, no sign of a single tear being shed. I open my mouth, but before I can ask a question, Kindell rushes forward.

Enveloping me in a tight, perfume-scented hug, she rocks me back and forth.

"Thank you—it doesn't feel like enough, but thank you, Nory."

Together we stumble into my front room, and the other women follow, shutting my door behind them with a thud. Kindell releases me, and I can take stock of the women now inside my home. A few of them I've met over the years to repair their clothes or make alterations for their husbands. There is a variety of ages at play here, too: an aging farmer's wife with deep wrinkles along her eyes and mouth, dressed in a frayed frock, to a young merchant's bride with a sparkling wedding band and gaunt face.

All of the women look at me with hope in their eyes.

"What's going on?" I ask, even as I know the answer.

It's plain as day to see why they've all come here. I feel Eryx's presence in the back room, ready to pounce if necessary. Kindell takes my hand and squeezes it, clearly a spokesperson for this mismatched group.

"Word of my husband's *untimely* demise came early this morning."

Her words are clipped with no sign of emotion. Not that I can blame her. The memory of her husband's hands along my body and his lecherous words makes bile churn in my stomach. An awful man—he is where he deserves to be now.

That's why I don't even attempt to offer condolences; none of the women seems to mind. The hope in their gazes only intensifies.

"Everyone in this town has been on edge since the livestock started dying. Now with three deaths in the span of three days —a few of the men in town think there's some sort of killer on the loose." Icy fingernails rake down my spine, but Kindell merely grins. "Of course, I told them all it was nonsense—that my husband had been foolish to travel alone and I had warned him not to that night in front of many of his friends. Still, they didn't believe me and seemed intent on launching some sort of investigation."

Kindell gestures towards the women around here.

"These are all of their wives who attest they are each as cruel as my husband was—and would be happy to see them meet a fate similar to his."

That's what this is—a warning and a solution. These women want me to liberate them the same way I had Isabelle and Kindell. This is also their way of telling me that if I don't take care of these men, they will eventually uncover my crimes and come after me.

If I were smart, I'd leave today. I have enough money to travel—Eryx could guide me at least to a nearby port and start over somewhere far away. If the men of this village are already onto me, killing any more would be foolish.

Kindell must sense my hesitation. Her eyes grow serious as the silence stretches.

"Please, Nory, help them like you helped me. They have plenty of money to pay you," she urges. "With fewer men around to ask questions, there is less of a chance you will ever be discovered for helping us. All these women will keep your secret."

I bite my lip, conflicting feelings warring inside me.

The farmer's wife looks at me—her voice is meek and unassuming.

"Help us, please. These men are loyal to each other—they'll pay someone to hunt you down if you try to flee. You'll never be safe from them unless you kill them."

I sigh. As much as I hate to admit it, she's right. These men combined have enough coin to pay one of the sell-swords that frequent the tavern to track me for the rest of my days. I won't live in constant fear—checking over my shoulder, waiting to be found out.

While I have Eryx now, will he always be there for me? A part of me still can't shake that he's keeping something from me and that our time together is coming to an end. Without him, I would have no protection should anyone come seeking retribution.

However, more than that, as I stare into the haunted faces of the women around me, I know I have to aid them. I'm the only hope they've got.

"Fine. I'll help you all."

A soft cheer goes up as the women around me visibly relax. One by one, they each hand over heavy sacks of gold coins— the farmer's wife extends a bag of grain and a few copper pieces, and I take them along with the other payments, easing her worry over the meager sum. After collecting their payments, each one provides me with a description of their husbands and where they typically frequent.

Once the last woman leaves with her thanks still echoing in the air, I rise from my work table. I don't need to confirm with Eryx that he will help me. He offered to slaughter all the men in this town this morning, and the more I think about it, the more I realize that won't be too far off from what we are doing.

This will be quite the undertaking. Excitement pulses in my veins, and even though it is wrong, I can't help but be eager to see Eryx in action again. Who knew I had such bloodlust of my own? He and I truly make the perfect team.

Tonight, we will be unleashed on the Snowlands again. I can hardly wait. Throughout the morning, I find myself counting down the minutes until the sun finally sets.

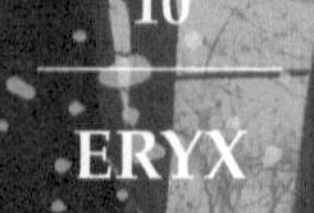

10

ERYX

These past days have left me on the edge between agony and bliss.

Each day, I am in pain, forcing myself to keep away from Nory so that she can get her work done. However, a male like me can only hold off for so long. After only a handful of hours spent prowling the shadows of her home or the surrounding forest, I slink back into her house and take her atop whatever clothing she's mending. Her fingernails bite into my back as I swallow her high-pitched moans.

Each time I feel her come around my cock and I fill her with my seed, the madness inside of me intensifies. Once we have come down from our shaking climaxes, it's not long before she's forgoing her work in favor of me wringing pleasure from every inch of her body.

Nighttime is when we unleash our full desire.

Once my bloodlust is satisfied by our latest victim, I turn that primal edge on Nory. She meets my depraved lust with her own, allowing me to drink from her before taking her in countless maddening ways. I feast from her neck as well as between her thighs, drinking down her sweet honey from both places. With her blood inside me, our passion reaches new peaks.

The jealousy I feel as I watch her play her role burns hotly. Now, the men she lures don't even get the chance to touch her before I pounce on them—ripping their throats out before claiming her beside their corpses. I've taken her roughly more places than I can count.

We've fucked in old barnes where her moans echo through the rafters. I've lain atop a fresh pile of snow deep in the grave-yard as she looms above me naked. Her breasts bounce as she rides me under the pale moon. Each time we come together, my heart lifts, believing this will be it. The time we finally succumb to the unspoken truth lurking between us and fulfill my maker's demand.

Each time, I am left disappointed by her refusal to confess. However, that feeling of discontentment quickly dissipates as she looks at me with trust and adoration in her eyes. Each time it makes me want to prove myself more—clearly, I am not doing enough to earn the feelings I desire from her.

I am not ignorant of the passing of time. My maker's dead-line looms—I've wasted too much time. Before, days passed slowly, agonizingly so. With Nory, time moves in the blink of an eye. I'll seek her out at noon, and by the time I feel wrung out from pleasure, it's nearly midnight.

Despite the passage of days, I can feel a difference within me as well. Even gorging myself on those despicable males and Nory's sweet blood, the hunger inside me never abates. My bones feel brittle, on the verge of breaking. Even my magic has begun to wane, simple tasks require more concentration than I've ever used.

Nory has noticed the change in me as well. Her verdant eyes snag on the increasing pallor of my skin. There is concern in her gaze and a trepidation in her touch as if she knows—even though it is impossible. I will not tell her and risk my maker's wrath. All I can hope is that today will be the day she fully submits to me, and my maker's bargain will be fulfilled.

My maker's demands plague my every thought—only silenced when I am deep inside Nory, just like I am now.

Our latest victim—a merchant with his silken cloak sodden with blood—lies in a heap along the alley wall. He was forgotten the moment his body hit the ground. With eager hands, Nory pulled me towards her, licking his blood from my tongue and placing my hands onto her soft body. I've skillfully arranged her over a weather-worn barrel deep in the shadows.

The scarlet hem of her dress has been hiked up around her hips. The supple mounds of her ass glow in the moonlight. Her stocking-clad thighs are wide, exposing both her little pink holes to my gaze. I retreat my hips, hissing as her hot, wet pussy greedily tries to suck me back within her.

Nory whimpers, pushing back to try to sheath me inside her. After a moment of reprieve, I slam back into her with a grunt. My hips bounce off her ass, and she coats me in more delicious arousal. The scent of her cunt swirls around me and kindles my *lifefire*. Her teeth sink into my palm as I silence her screams of pleasure with my hand.

The sounds of our slapping bodies echo in the silent night. A storm has moved in, and a whipping wind conceals most of our noise. Nory's blunt nails dip into the wooden top of the barrel that rocks with each of my hard thrusts. Leaning down, I lick up her neck as my mouth finds her ear.

"Look at how desperate you are for my cock, Nory. We just killed someone, and you're too greedy to be fucked to care. Naughty girl. If you weren't so perfect, I'd have to punish you."

She tightens like a vice on my cock, and I grin. The ridges of my length drag inside her perfect heat.

"You'd like to be punished, wouldn't you?"

Nory nods frantically, but it's not enough. Lifting my hand from her hip, I quickly smack her ass, watching color bloom on her pale skin. Nory moans into my palm, her thighs beginning to tremble. I spank her again—it didn't take me long to learn Nory like a bit of pain with her pleasure.

"Use your words," I command, removing my palm from her mouth to snatch back her hair.

Curving her spine, she bends perfectly, allowing me to fuck her even deeper. The head of my cock butts up against her womb and urges me to spill inside of her. Not yet, I have to wait until she's come, even if it seems impossible to hold on. With her red hair wrapped around my fist, I pull until I know she feels a prick of pain.

Her eyes stare at me, glossy with pleasure.

"Punish me, Eryx. Use me however you want. I need it."

Her words are broken up by soft moans. Sucking my thumb into my mouth, I reach between her pink cheeks and press my finger against the tight muscles of her back entrance—Nory squeals, thrashing in my grasp and rewarding me with a fresh rush of wetness.

"Even if I fucked you here?"

My thumb breaks through the tight ring and pushes deep. Her breath catches in her throat as she begins to tremble. Her peak is close, and I savor it.

"Well, Nory? Answer me."

"I—I—"

"You sound so pitiful," I sigh. "Are you close to coming?"

"Yes!"

"Good. Give me an answer, and I'll make you come."

Nory swallows and looks at me over her shoulder. She is more beautiful with every passing day, especially with her pink cheeks and tears of desperation drying along them. Her freckles are like stars decorating her pale face. Biting her full lips, I watch her body bow in complete supplication to my thrusts.

"Take my ass, Eryx. It belongs to you," she gasps. "Now, please, make me come."

I chuckle darkly and thrust my thumb back into her ass, delighting in her broken moan. My other hand leaves her hair and sneaks under her hips to rub circles on her greedy clit. Her body locks down on mine, and her mouth opens in a silent scream.

"Come for me, Nory. Coat me in that sweet fucking come while I flood your pretty cunt with my spend."

I retreat my hips and power into her once, twice, until the base of my spine tingles. On the third and final thrust, I push deep. Her ass cushions my hips, and I come deep inside of her. My sticky release squelches between us and falls to the dirt floor of the alley.

Pleasure kindles my *lifefire* to another level. It makes me wonder how I ever lived without it before—without Nory. Even if my undoing wasn't looming, there is no way that I could continue without her. She is it for me—forever.

I can't survive without her. I won't.

Once she has come down from her orgasm, I cuddle Nory's trembling body into mine. Glancing down, I take in our victim one last time. He was the final victim—no other women have come seeking Nory's help. Truth be told, men have been leaving the Snowlands at a rapid rate.

With no more plots to hatch, I wonder how to satiate Nory's own bloodlust. She has the heart of a killer in the body of a goddess. There's an edge to her—a desire to watch those who deserve to suffer—that has been hidden by her tender disposition. Even with all the money she's earned from helping the women of this town, monetary fulfillment will never truly satisfy her.

Nory pulls back, a tired smile on her lips. My dead heart urges to beat along with her pounding one. In the moonlight and freshly fucked, she is gorgeous. I can smell my scent mixing with her sweetness, and my cock begins to harden again. Once we're back in her cottage, I'll be counting down the seconds until I'm inside of her again.

A wicked thought flows through me as I stare down into her trusting eyes. What if the reason I have not earned her confession is that she has become too comfortable in our routine? There is no more mystery between us—the sharpest edges of the monster I used to be have been dulled by her. What if I need to show her the depth of my devotion so she is encouraged to meet it with her own?

I've been playing by her rules this whole time. Going wherever she bid me and doing whatever she said—and I've enjoyed every moment. What if I no longer gave her a choice? What if I took her deep into *The Woods* and fucked her endlessly until her confession came out as a broken sob of pleasure?

The image of her shaking and desperate—vowing to be mine in no uncertain terms—makes me burn hotter. I'm lost to the depraved fantasy as we leave the alley and quickly travel back to her cottage. It is wrong—I couldn't do something like that...could I?

With the old oak door swinging shut behind us, I watch Nory hang her cloak by the fire. Her green eyes find mine. Exhaustion weighs her down; if I were to take her, she'd hardly fight me.

With a yawn, she leans against the wall.

"As much as I am glad to have helped these women, I'm happy it's over now. Doing two in one night definitely took a toll."

I nod, unsure that if I open my mouth, I won't confess to wanting to steal her away. If I took her now, she would be mad—but would she really fight me for long? I can give her pleasure in my embrace and protection from the dangers of this world. Even as I think it, maybe it would be wise to talk to her.

Nory has always managed to surprise me. If I told her of my wish to take her away, maybe she would go willingly.

Our time together is coming to an end. This may be the only chance I have to take her from this stagnant environment and thrust her into one where there is only me. If she understands how desperate I am for her, it could be just the thing to break through any final barrier keeping her confession at bay.

And if it's not, I will spend our final hours together in total bliss. My primal nature stirs after a deep slumber at the thought of keeping her. Even if she tries to flee, I'll capture her and pin her beneath me until she is begging for my cock once again.

I shake myself and decide to go with a reasonable approach.

"Nory," I say, crossing over to her and taking her in my arms. She comes willingly, and that gives me enough hope to press on. "I've been thinking...we should leave the Snowlands. Together. We can make a home—just the two of us. Somewhere far away from here. You have more than enough money to leave this all behind. I do as well—enough to get us a house deep in *The Woods* where I am more powerful and can protect you better."

Her lush mouth parts. Blinking green eyes up at me, she is quiet as a dozen emotions flash across her face. My hands tremble along her back as hope dances through my veins.

Only to be shattered in an instant.

"No." The word is said so softly I barely hear it. Before she says anything else, she's pushing away from me and taking a step back. "No—I—I couldn't. My life is here—I just killed all those men to keep it. Not to mention my responsibilities. Here I have a purpose. What would I have if I left?"

"Me." I reach for her, but she sidesteps me. "You would have me. Don't you want that?"

Desperation claws at my stomach. With the distance she's putting between us, I realize that I've played my hand wrong, and if I don't act decisively now, I could lose her forever. Have I truly misread her so completely?

There is a brief moment of hope as a look of longing dances in her eyes. Silence stretches as if she is considering it despite her quick refusal. Then, as if a sheet of ice has encased her, all warmth leaves Nory. Her skin turns paler as her eyes turn stoic.

"I always expected you to leave. Especially with our bargain complete." Her voice is odd—breathy—not that of the confident woman I've come to know. "Now I have the means to live my life the way I wanted to before my mother's passing—*alone*."

My eyes roam over Nory as I stare at her. I've heard her words, but they don't make sense. These past weeks together could not have been a lie—she promised me forever every time I touched her. Now she is claiming otherwise, that our time together was fleeting. I've felt her heart and tasted her soul. Nory is mine.

With the undoing looming, I have no choice but to give in to my madness. A desperate male will do anything to secure the thing he wants most in this world. I've never wanted anything as much as I want Nory. I let the mania devour me, and the monster I am floats to the surface. Her body jerks as she watches the change come over me.

While I may look the same, the male before her is different from the one she's come to know. He can taste her lies and will stop at nothing to have her.

A dark chuckle permeates my chest. Nory backs up a step, but I quickly come upon her.

"You can't mean that."

A stubborn tilt to her chin and the defiance in her eyes is the only indicator that the real Nory—my Nory—hasn't been devoured by her icy denial.

"I do," she spits.

Another chuckle leaves me as I grasp her upper arm.

"You expect me to believe you've been biding your time—

waiting for me to go—with my seed still drying on your thighs." I inhale deeply, licking my lips and delighting in the faint trace of her I find there. Her cheeks darken as she tries to free herself from me. "I know you, Nory—better than you know yourself. I'm the only one who's seen the real you—tasted her too."

She trembles as I lower my face to the juncture of her neck and shoulder. Licking up her throat, my lips find their way to her ear.

"Maybe I just need to fuck you again so you remember."

Nory rears back, fire burning her eyes. Her chest rises and falls. The hard peaks of her nipples bead along her dress. I can scent the delicious state of her pussy. Her anger is real, but so is her desire. Good, I'll just—

A sharp knock at the door breaks through our tense silence. She glares up at me, and I reluctantly release her. The quicker she gets rid of whoever is at her doorstep, the better. She won't try to flee or alert them of my presence here—of that I'm certain.

"This conversation isn't over," I growl, before slinking into the shadows.

"Just stay hidden," she hisses back.

Throwing me one last exasperated look, Nory turns the brass knob and thrusts open the door. The scent from the other side sets my body on edge—it is distinctly male. From my hidden vantage point, I can see an older man there. His clothes are in disarray, with a few spots of blood marking the collar of his shirt. A fresh gash has been carved into his cheek. In his hand is the thin upper arm of an elderly woman.

Nory's color has gone pale as the man stomps into her home, dragging the older woman along with him.

"What is the meaning of all this?" Nory demands.

Tossing the old woman to the floor, she hits the ground with a cry. The man's hand wraps around the handle of a dagger as he points a bony finger at Nory.

"Don't play dumb with me," he barks. "My friends—you've killed them all. Everyone said I was crazy—that bad luck had just befallen them. Well, I wasn't buying that. Knew something worse was at play."

Unsheathing his dagger, he points it at the older woman. There is a trail of blood leaking from her temple and soaking the collar of her shirt.

"Didn't take her long to confess after a few hours of persuasion," he sneers. "Her husband told me just how to keep her line should he not be around to do it."

The older woman has gone deathly pale.

"I'm so sorry, Nory. Forgive me, I never meant to—"

"Be quiet, you old hag!" he shouts.

The man's eyes shift on Nory, turning from angry to lecherous in an instant. My blood boils as I watch him drift closer to her. The deadly tip of his knife points directly at her. Nory remains still, her eyes never leaving him. My brave, beautiful Nory—she knows there's no reason to fear him. Not with me here.

He assured his death the moment he walked in here.

"As for you, *Nory*," he sneers. "You will die for killing my friends. I've told the other men in this town who haven't left in fear and are already on their way."

Looking her up and down, he bares his yellow teeth as he licks his lips.

"I'll have a little fun with you." His hands fall to the buckle of his trousers. "Before the others arrive and want a turn."

The old woman on the floor begins crying in earnest as the man takes another step forward. Nory's green eyes fly to where I'm hiding—able to find me even when I'm cloaked in shadow —and that's all the urging I need.

Emerging with a growl, the man doesn't even have the chance to scream before I pin him to the wall and bite into his throat. Hot blood flows over my lips and down my throat. The older woman screams at the sight. I'm vaguely aware of her rising from the floor and stumbling out the door—her sounds of terror echoing in the night.

I rip out the man's throat and spit it on the ground. His body falls in a heap at my feet, and red blood soaks Nory's floorboards. Blood spills down my chest and over my armor. From through the open door, I can hear voices approaching quickly.

Whirling towards Nory, her cheeks are pink as I step towards her trembling body.

"It's not safe for you here." I hold her by the waist, savoring the heat of her body. "You are coming with me. Now."

Nory swallows loudly before shaking her head.

"No." Her protest is weak.

The voices outside get louder, and if we don't leave now, more blood will be spilled. As much as I would relish it, I'd much rather have Nory all to myself than taste one more vile drop of blood.

"Have it your way."

My fingers tighten on her waist before hoisting her up and over my shoulder. Turning from the carnage in her front room, I push through the open door and feel the night air envelope us. Slinking into the darkness unseen, Nory comes to life on my shoulder. She screams and beats along my back. Bucking and thrashing in my grip, her attempts to escape me are futile.

The Woods loom up ahead. My steps never falter as I walk towards it, a smile playing on my lips.

"Finally."

11

—

NORY

Fighting him is futile, but I still try.

Thrashing against his firm hold, I pound the hard muscles of his back until the sides of my hands ache. The rushing of the night wind covers my screams of discontent. Eryx moves quickly—something I was already well aware of, but to experience it firsthand is something else. In a matter of seconds, my cottage is no more than a speck of dust littering the horizon. The thicket of trees quickly consumes us until all traces of the Snowlands are blighted.

All of my belongings remain behind in the house. Every memory I have left behind in an instant. As the night swirls around us, my life flashes before my eyes—desperate as I am to uncover a happy memory, none surface.

There is only that house in which my mother toiled away at the workbench—permanently bent fingers and a hunched back. Withering away day by day until illness had taken her. The workload that had stolen her youth was thrust on my shoulders. My own life is a series of unfortunate events—play-time cut short as a small child so I could tend to my long list of chores. No time for teenage courting when the steady stream of customers never abated.

It was never a life—it was only suffering.

Still, it was all I had known my entire life. Working in hopes of gaining financial freedom and independence has always been a lofty goal. Even with the means I acquired from helping the women of this town, would I have ever left if Eryx hadn't taken me? If my crimes had never been uncovered, would I still be in that cottage, toiling away until illness befell me just as it had my mother?

A gasp leaves me as I realize with a start that I haven't been to her grave since the night I summoned Eryx. A place I haunted like a faithful phantom I had all but forgotten. That is how it has been since he came into my life. From the moment he touched me, I knew my days of solidarity were over. The fantasy of my future now included him—the two of us traveling together hand in hand. Finding solstice in each other's touch every night, and seeing each new day as a gift we would spend together.

It was what my heart longed for—despite my protests and rejection of him, he had seen past it and taken me. Fear makes my emotions tangle in a dark web. Instead of examining them, I decide to continue my fight instead. He won't let me go. He's stolen my choice to flee just like I needed him to. If not forced to confront these feelings, I never would.

That doesn't mean I won't put up a fight even if I can't win. I smack his back relentlessly. Bucking myself along his shoulder, I scream and try to wriggle off him. *The Woods* are dark as we pass through them. Eryx guides us over thick roots and jagged boulders.

"Let me go!" I screech, trying to claw through his cloak.

I kick my legs and Eryx freezes. My breathing is ragged as I take in the deserted clearing. At our feet is a thick patch of dark grass, outlined by pale stones and an assortment of low-hanging branches.

Hooking me under my hips, Eryx hefts me from his shoulders. I fight his grip and clatter to the soft ground. The moisture of the grass soaks through my cotton dress before I can jump up. With an exasperated sigh, I turn from him, determined to storm off even if I don't have a clue in the world which way town is, and that it would be unwise to return.

My rational brain is not thinking as I stomp away, but Eryx is quick, snagging me around the arm and dragging me back.

He brackets me in his iron grip. His eyes are unreadable, the fire in them a dull orange.

"Let me go," I repeat through clenched teeth. "You've kidnapped me, and I won't stand for it."

A wicked thrill shoots through me. It's the same thrill I feel watching him kill those who deserve it. His show of force will always elicit pleasure from me, even when it shouldn't be welcome. His apparent desperation is evident. All this time, he's been patient with me—letting me set the pace between us. Now he's snapped, and knowing I have the power to make this centuries-old being break is a heady thought.

Eryx bares his teeth in a grin.

"You won't be standing for long."

I gasp, pulling back against his hold even as wetness pools between my thighs.

"Unhand me, you—you monster!"

Eryx chuckles, bringing me flush against his body. The hard press of his cock against my stomach causes a moan to fall from my lips. His midnight scent wraps around me like a blanket. The rigid plates of his armor tease my nipples.

"I've been too soft with you," he chides. "Been too wary that if you glimpsed the beast you've taken into your bed, you would run from me."

My hands rest on his chest, frozen. I have the chance to push him off, but why am I not taking it?

"It seems I'm adept at catching you, my beautiful prey. Your words mean little when I can scent the delicious state of your pussy."

Heat engulfs my cheeks as I rub my thighs together. His crude words inflame my lust even though my mind tells me not to give in and fight. How much of a fight can I really put up when in my heart I want him to capture me and never let me go?

Eryx's fingers cup my chin and force my face up towards his.

"Entertain me, prey. Tell me you don't want me."

My heart pounds against my ribs, and I lick my lips.

"I don't want you." The words taste like poison on my tongue.

Eryx's smile only widens.

"Liar." His lips skim over mine, making me ache. "Tell me you want to be freed."

My fingers dig into his chest, flexing to pull him closer.

"Let me go," I sigh. My protest is as weak as my resistance.

Eryx's lips press firmly against mine, and I moan into his mouth. His hand falls down my back to cup my ass, pulling me flush against his hard cock. I rock back and forth against it, swallowing his hiss of pleasure.

"Even your lies taste sweet," he murmurs against my mouth.

Something sparks inside of me—a need to show that he hasn't won just yet. His mouth descends on mine, but before our kiss can commence, I snag his bottom lip between my teeth. With force, I bite down, tasting his dark, metallic blood. Eryx growls, pulling back to lick at the wound. His eyes blaze red, and I use this moment of surprise to pull away.

Making a break for it, I'm free from his arms and race towards the nearest opening of trees. Eryx is hot on my heels as he rushes after me. Cold air stings my cheeks and the tips of my ears. My heart pounds in my chest, and with each uneven step I will him to capture me.

The realization nearly makes me stumble.

I want to be caught and kept—I want Eryx. All of my problems and worries vanish when he is around. I trust him to care for me and keep me safe. For so long, I've been fighting all alone, and now I have someone who will do it all for me. My heart and mind clash, shattering into a million pieces. They knit back together as one, and it belongs entirely to Eryx.

There is no point in fighting it any longer. I am right where I'm supposed to be.

My slipper snags on an exposed root and kicks my legs out from underneath me. I brace myself for the impending fall until I feel two strong hands wrapping around me. Eryx saves me—just as he always does—from harm. I'm crushed against his hard chest as he quickly backs me up into the base of a massive tree. My feet leave the ground as he holds me aloft.

"Did you really think you could escape me?" he snarls into my face.

His pale skin glows, and madness dances along the flames in his eyes.

"There is nowhere you can go that I will not follow. Your face, your scent, and your soul are imprinted on my bones. Only death could separate us."

Desperation drips from every word. Each time he touches me is more unrestrained. These past few days, I've noticed the change in him—whiter skin and sharper edges to his face. Whatever plight he's suffering from, he has not shared. If only he would tell me I could help him solve it.

It is a stark reminder of the fear I've felt since we were first together under the moon. Our time is limited, and each breath spent fighting seems like a waste. I have no wish to deny us both any longer.

We stare at each other for one final moment of peace before

we give in to the primal nature of our desire. Lifting my chin, I brush my lips over his.

"Good," I say, taking his mouth with mine in a bruising kiss.

Eryx snarls against me. Our kiss turns into a frantic fight of clashing teeth and twisting tongues. His taste envelopes me along with his scent. I give in to the battle and let him overwhelm me.

Eryx's hands roam over me completely, squeezing and caressing every inch of skin. My breath hitches as his hands find the neckline of my dress. The sound of tearing fabric causes me to pull back. Wetness coats my thighs as Eryx rips the fabric clean down the center. My shift is given the same treatment until I am completely naked, save for a pair of wool stockings, before his hungry gaze—the hard bark of the tree scores against my back as he pushes me against it.

His mouth is on mine again in a fleeting moment. Warm lips kiss down my jaw and neck, licking over the spot scarred by his bite. He groans as he inhales and continues down my body. The wet glide of his tongue on my nipples causes my heart to hammer against my ribs. He pays each breast attention before kissing lower.

Licking over the freckles along my stomach, his hands fall to my hips, pinning me in place. Hot breath ghosts over my pussy, and I toss my head back against the tree. Eryx chuckles as he lifts my left leg and positions it over his shoulder. Spread before his hungry gaze, I can only sigh.

"Denying me has made you deliciously wet, Nory."

The first glide of his tongue up my slit is nearly my undoing. I moan into the darkness. The moonlight highlights his pale flesh. I whimper as his dark tongue spears into my entrance and drives deep. It reaches and pushes—a perfect mirror to the way he fucks me with his cock. His face rubs back and forth against my clit. My hands fall to his head and hold him tight to me.

His mouth makes delightful, sloppy sounds as he feasts on me. The world around us is quiet, as if we are the only two beings alive left in this world. Moans fall from my lips in rapid succession as he continues to work me. My hips grind desperately for more friction. His fingers dig into my ass.

The tip of his tongue tickles that hidden spot inside me, and I erupt. Throwing my head back, I scream my pleasure as my pussy locks around his thrusting tongue. I ride him through each wave of my pleasure. Licking me clean, Eryx kisses up my trembling body until he reaches my mouth. Pulling me from the tree, he cradles me against him. My legs wrap around his waist as he lowers us to the soft grass.

Wickedness flares to life inside me again. Never breaking our kiss, I use my strength to roll us until I am positioned on top of his body. Smiling against his mouth, I delight in my taste and realize I've never given him the same pleasure. That will be rectified this instant.

"My turn," I sigh, kissing along his jaw.

His soft skin is revealed as we work together to shed his old cloak and heavy armor. I kiss over his chest and drag my nipples along his stomach. In the moonlight, he looks otherworldly. His face is contorted in painful pleasure as his eyes blaze. Shuffling down his body, soft grass meets my knees as my mouth looms over his proud length. Already it is straining and dripping sticky seed.

"Go on," Eryx commands. "Take me into that pretty mouth of yours."

Gripping him in my fist, I give him a soft pump.

"Fuck," he snarls. "Again."

I do as he says, a willing submissive. More moisture leaks from the tip, and I lick it off with my tongue. His salty flavor delights me. Liquid arousal flows down my thighs as I lick over his head again.

"Am I doing good? I've never done this before."

I bat my lashes at him, the picture of innocent curiosity. Eryx nods, his hands flexing in the ground beside him.

"Perfect."

I blush at his compliment and give a proud shake of my shoulders. Lowering myself, I lick up the side of his length. His ridges dig into my tongue. Eryx's muscles tighten, and his breathing turns ragged. Encouraged by his reaction, I take him fully into my mouth.

The stretch of him burns. My tongue glides along him until he bumps the back of my throat. Tears blur my vision as I pull back. My hand works him in time with my mouth as I take him deep again. More seed leaks into my mouth as I suck.

Slippery with my saliva, I can work him deep and deep with each suck. Eryx's hips lift, and he slips further down my throat. A chorus of curses slips from his mouth as he begins to pant. His hands lift to my head and hold me firm to his hard cock.

"Fuck, Nory. So perfect choking on my cock—take it, my beautiful prey. Work for my come and I'll reward you with it."

I moan against his length, reaching between my thighs to rub circles on my clit. I'm desperate for any sort of relief. Doubling my efforts, I work him deeper and faster. My nose brushes against his hips as I suck him. My hand barely wraps around him as I continue to pump.

Eryx gives a broken moan as he comes fully off the ground. His cock hardens even more against my tongue, and I gag on his cock as he spills a torrent of hot seed down my throat. Tears sting my eyes and flow down my cheeks. I swallow down as best I can, but stickiness coats my lips and chin. One final spray lands across my lips, and I lick it off.

More tears fall from my eyes as my own climax approaches. I make a keening sound, and Eryx's eyes blaze to awareness. In the next moment, I am flat on my back with him surging between my splayed thighs. His seed coats my face and chest, and I must look like a mess.

Eryx doesn't care as he leans down to capture my mouth. With one hard thrust, he sheaves himself fully inside of me. I'm still sensitive from my first orgasm. My body is already racing towards its peak. Bracing one hand above my head, Eryx fucks into me ruthlessly. We share moans and grunts as our bodies slap together.

"Tightest cunt in all the land. I had to kill to earn it—I'll kill to keep it."

"Yes!" I scream.

The ridges of his cock drag along my sensitive walls. My hands fall to his hips and pull him forcefully against me—desperate to have him as close as possible.

"Faster." My words are slurred with pleasure. "Fuck me, Eryx. Please!"

My revenant growls as he thrusts harder, embedding himself within me. His pale cock disappears into my wet, pink flesh in rapid succession. I feel the stretch of him in a maddening way. I want more—I want it all.

"Squeeze that little pussy on my cock again, and I'll flood it with seed. It'll drip out of you for hours." He chuckles harshly. "If you're good, maybe I'll lick it out of you."

His words heighten my pleasure. Flames lick at my bare skin, and my muscles tighten.

There is no part of me he doesn't own. With each thrust, our souls weave together. My heart calls to him as if we have known each other for centuries. We are one. Eternity beckons me, and I reach forward to claim it. Eryx is the revenant who saved me. He is the monster who protects me. He is the male I lo—

"Eryx!" I scream.

My pussy locks onto his cock as he fucks me, and I am tossed off the mountain of my climax. Fire washes over my skin, and each nerve sings with pleasure. My nails rake down his back as he groans and freezes over me. My pussy is filled to the brim with his hot seed. It leaks from between our bodies and hits the grass below us with a hiss.

Eyrx pumps into me one final time, ensuring I've taken all his spend. My body relaxes enough to let him slip from me. A fresh rush of our mingling releases coats my thighs as he rolls me onto my side and into his chest. His hands skim up my bare back.

In the moonlight, I take in the pallor of his skin. The bones underneath look darker than usual, his eyes more hollow. I trace the thin skin there. He must need to feed—that is all.

"Does this mean you've given yourself to me?" he asks, voice rough from his cries of pleasure.

I smile and nestle deep into him.

"Yes. I'm afraid you're stuck with me."

Eryx chuckles before breaking off on a harsh cough. The air around us turns frigid as his whole body tenses. I pull back to look at him and cry out—his pale skin begins to dry and flake off his bones. The fire in his eyes dulls into embers.

"Eryx?" I ask, panicking. "What's going on?"

He coughs again, falling onto his back as more skin begins to wither and crumble away. I crawl over him, smoothing the dampness from his brow. In the dying flames of his eyes, I see a variety of emotions. Anger, sadness, and finally longing—each one encases my heart in ice. The organ gives a painful squeeze as I take in the sight of him.

I need to call for help—I need to—

"Fate is cruel—if I had more time, I'd tell you everything."

His voice is a broken whimper, and tears blur my vision.

"What's happening?" I demand.

His smile is small. The skin rips from his cheeks and jawbone.

"I'm out of time. I—" He breaks off with a cough. Lifting a trembling hand to my cheek, the bones of his fingers press into my skin. "You were my gift, Nory. To have you, even if it was too brief, was more than I deserved. You are good, beautiful, and kind. My heart is yours. So is my soul...forever."

A haunting death rattle falls from his mouth and shakes the ground. Color leeches from his skin until it is all crumbling and ashen. The flames of his eyes flicker in the night breeze before extinguishing. Despair punches through the ground and drags me down into its depths.

"No!" I scream. "This can't be it—there has to be another way. Please!"

I scream up at the moon, my hands falling to his chest as if I can hold him in this world.

"This can't be happening. We've barely had any time, you can't take him!"

Tears fall in hot streams down my cheeks. My fingers tunnel through his thin skin until they brush the smooth bones underneath. Bile floods my stomach as I look at him. This can't be it —our story can't be over—not when there are still so many things left unsaid.

"Please," I whimper. "Don't take him. I love him."

My confession echoes around us in the empty clearing. It is the truth—I love Eryx. Now that I've admitted it, I can't pinpoint the moment I fell in love with him, perhaps from our very first meeting or when he agreed to help me. Whenever it was, it's been building all this time, consuming me with its ferocity. I love him, I *love* him.

If he is not in this world, then neither will I be.

A pale blue spark kindles in his gaze, but is extinguished with his next breath. His chest does not rise again. Anguish floods me as I fall to a heap atop his crumbling body. I sob into the darkness. Painful, beseeching cries of anguish rip through my lungs. I'm cold—so, so cold. Every inch of my body is in pain. My heart has stopped beating, and my soul reaches for the one it was tied to.

I don't know how long I cry over his corpse until I finally

hear it. It's soft at first—a distant humming that rises into a loud crescendo. Metal coats the air and burns my throat. Looking up, all I can see through my tears is pale moonlight. It burns brighter and brighter until it floods through the thicket of trees around us. The light makes my tender eyes burn as it illuminates the clearing.

Eryx's still body becomes even more visible. The state of his decay tears at my heart, and a sob chokes me. A breeze whispers over my wet cheeks, soft as a touch. Before me, the bright light condenses into one form. Neither male nor female, it is just a pulsing being of dazzling light.

A voice that is both loud and quiet echoes from the trees.

"He's done it—my final child. I knew he was special from the moment I crafted him—it's why I named him. Gentler than the others—he felt deeply, longed for companionship like none of the others had before. He was my last hope for them to be more."

This otherworldly being's words are nonsense.

"What—what are you?" I ask.

"A demon to some, a god to others. Titles are so fickle. What matters now is that I was right and that I keep my promises."

Confusion steals my voice, but the being doesn't seem forthcoming with answers anyway. Light flows from their form and covers Eryx's body in glittering brightness. I gasp as I watch his skin return, thicker than before. The sharp angles of his face are smoothed out. Eyelids form over his sockets, framed with dark lashes.

Eryx is still monstrous—only now a bit more solid. Glancing up at the figure, their words tickle my ears.

"He will sleep for a time. When he rises, he will be like he was, but not completely. Neither alive nor dead, but a third thing. Immortal but with the soul of a human." Their light grows brighter, and I nearly have to look away. "Have him feed from you if you wish to join him in eternity. The choice is yours, Norella."

With that, the figure is gone. Shadows overtake their light. Staring down at Eryx, I watch his strong chest rise and fall. Hope threads my broken heart back together. I lay my head against his tear-soaked chest. Wrapping my arms around his middle, he is warmer than ever before.

I can hardly make sense of all I've witnessed. Eryx's death, telling him I love him, and now this being—this—I don't even know what it was. I'm not sure I can handle any more surprises, but as my ear rests against his heart, I'm greeted by its rhythmic pounding for the first time. I can't help but let out a watery laugh.

"Wake up," I whisper. "Please, Eryx. Wake up."

My pleas are whispered against his chest until the first rays of sunlight spill through the trees.

For a moment, there was only light.

Stark, unyielding light. It was cold wherever I went. The only solace had been Nory's scent—in this between realm, she was here. I greedily drank it down, even if I no longer had a body. I could still feel the weight of her in my arms—the softness of her skin.

I had been so close to getting everything I wanted, and now, just like the rest of my kind, I had been undone. This is all I will be now, a ghost in this forsaken realm. A dark shelf for my soul to be put on and forgotten about as my corpse rots away in the land of the living.

The nothingness stretched—maybe that was my punishment. To be trapped in this nothingness, forced to live through the fading of my memories, rendering me nothing but an empty husk.

I should be grateful that I can at least remember myself and remember what I had, even if it was too brief.

Nory. My life, my heart, my love—I had loved her desperately from the first moment I saw her. I recognize that emotion now. It was foreign to my kind, and yet I had felt it all this time.

My maker knew it that day in *The Woods,* and that's why they had given me such an impossible bargain. I should curse them for making me different, for giving me the capacity to love, only for it to be ripped away.

Yet, I know that would be a lie. I would never be ungrateful for any part of caring for Nory. She was a gift in my final days— one I would give anything to experience just one last time. I long to run my fingers through her silken hair or hear her soft moans whispered against my ear. I can recall her voice and how she said my name. That is all lost to me now.

Still, her voice echoed around me, growing louder with each passing second. Nory's presence surrounded me. My name sounded from the nothingness. I tried to call for her but I had no mouth. Was this to be my punishment? To feel her this close and yet be unable to reach her?

I fought through it, pushing through the light with every ounce of my wretched soul. I followed the sound of her voice. Each time she spoke my name, it got clearer—I could scent her. The taste of her skin overwhelmed me. Continuing to push through the light, the nothingness fought back. The searing pain burned at my flesh as I raced against it and towards Nory.

The white light grew and grew until—in a flash—it faded, and all I saw were the branches of trees and the first rays of dawn. Darkness enveloped me and then revealed the scene again. The world around me kept cutting out before I realized what was interrupting my vision.

I was blinking. I was awake—alive.

Looking down at my body, my skin was pale but not gray. It was peachy. My frame was the same, even if my veins were now green and blue. Healthy blood flowed beneath the surface of my skin, and I was warm. Something thumped against my ribs —my heart, beating soundly. Racing like it never had before.

I was different. Alive and—

A gasp from beside me startles me. My heart thumps in my

chest at the sight of her huddled next to me. Clad only in my old cloak, Nory sits like a goddess in the morning light. Golden sun illuminates her sparkling auburn hair. Red-rimmed green eyes and a pink-tipped nose tell me she's been crying. Her freckles dance along her pale cheeks.

"Eryx," she whispers, reaching towards me.

Happiness slams into me as I wrap her in my arms and crush her to my chest. I absorb her sobs of pleasure and inhale her scent. Our warm, bare skin meets, and I've never felt like this in all the centuries I've been in this world. My head falls to the crook of her neck, and I inhale greedily.

The scent of her blood calls to me—making my mouth water. That answers that. I am not human, at least not entirely. My hunger for blood comes roaring to the forefront, reminding me how long it's been since I last fed. I'm something else now—still a revenant but changed.

Nory's forehead rests against mine as she smiles. Has she ever looked so beautiful? The sight of her makes my heart squeeze. This new organ is quite active; I'll have to get used to it.

"Your eyes," she sighs.

I reach towards them and end up poking one. Moisture coats my finger as it begins to blur. The sensation is unpleasant, and I'll have to remember how sensitive they are—Nory giggles before cupping my cheek.

"They're beautiful. Bright blue like the base of a flame."

I capture her hand, marveling over the softness of her skin and the calluses of her fingers. Each touch feels like a new exploration. Locking our fingers together, I stare into her gorgeous face.

"What happened? I was undone."

Nory swallows before nodding. A shiver wracks her body, and I hold her close.

"I can hardly explain it myself. Once you were gone," she

pauses, eyes brimming with tears, "there was this light. Bright white light."

I suck in a breath.

"My maker."

Nory's eyes go wide.

"Yes, they said you had done *it*. Whatever it is. Then they changed you into this new form right before my eyes."

My mouth goes dry as I stare at her. My maker did this? That can only mean one thing. One beautiful, impossible thing.

"You love me."

Nory gasps. With no threat of undoing, I can finally give her the explanation she deserves. Savoring her scent once more, I swallow soundly.

"The morning after you had taken me into your bed, I knew I had to find a way to earn more time. I knew I was dying—my undoing was only days away, and I was desperate. I sought out my maker and begged for more time with you. Told them I'd give anything."

"Eryx..."

"My maker told me that the only way they'd grant me the time I desired was if I could find a way to make you love me. If you could love a death omen, I would be spared my undoing and be given the future I begged them for. I couldn't tell you of our bargain or I would be undone in that very instant."

Nory is quiet for a moment. She bites her full lip as she looks at me over. Her hand trails along my shoulder, squeezing the muscles she grazes. I hold still, allowing her curious fingers to touch any part of me she wants. My cock is already stirring, but I will it to relax. There will be time for that later.

Her eyes snap back to mine, laden with raw emotion.

"You did all that...for me?"

My laugh is pure shock.

"There is nothing I wouldn't do for you. I love you, Nory. I'd endure the centuries of loneliness and hunger to be able to have you—even if only for a few days." My eyes burn into hers. "You are my heart and soul."

A conflicting look crosses her features.

"You're still immortal."

My hand caresses her soft cheek.

"I asked my maker to allow me to spend a human life with you. That is more than enough for me—once you pass from this world, so shall I."

I had made peace with my end some time ago. Immortality is meaningless without someone to share it with. I recognize that now. All I want is Nory for however long I have her. I'll safeguard her to ensure her human life is as long as possible. Once she is gone, I'll follow her into the next life—the next world—no matter where that is.

Licking her lips, Nory rests her palm over my thunderous heart.

"There's more." She hesitates. "When your maker changed you, they said you could turn me into what you are, so that we could both be immortal. All you'd need to do was bite me."

My whole body prickles with awareness. Nory immortal—the two of us seeing the world together without ever being parted. It sounds too good to be true. Maybe it is as Nory remains quiet, lost in her own thoughts.

"Would you want that?" I ask. "It is your choice. Always."

Closing her eyes, Nory inhales deeply. I wait with baited breath, unease raking its nails up my spine. She may love me, but that doesn't mean she wants to become like me. It is a lot to ask another to give up their humanity. I open my mouth to tell her as much, but her defiant eyes silence me.

Moisture beads along her lower lashes, but she blinks it away.

"For so long, all I wanted for myself was to make enough money so as not to be crushed under the weight of my work as my mother had been. I was certain I'd be forced into a marriage not of my choosing, so I was determined to lead a life of solitude. Longing for the day I could leave the Snowlands and live independently." Her lips curl into a breathtaking smile. "Now I see how foolish those dreams were. You came along and changed everything. My heart and soul belong to you, too, Eryx. I love you—and I never wish to be parted from you again. Not even in death."

My mouth descends on hers. With a sigh, we taste each other, and this kiss feels different—final. Our mouths slick over each other, and there's nothing more to say. Our decision has been made, and our life together starts now. No longer are we too lost and lonely wanderers, shackled to a life we could only endure. We have each other now. Forever.

With that in mind, my desperation abates as I take the time to savor her. I have forever to enjoy every inch of her thoroughly. To learn how best to kiss her until she's breathless or to make her come at the slightest brushing of my fingers. We have nothing but time now; there's only one last thing to do to ensure our forever.

However, I want the taste of her pussy on my tongue before her blood.

Unwrapping my cloak from her shoulders, I spread it out behind her and lower her to the ground. Nory sighs as I kiss down her body and settle between her hips. I waste no time diving between her slick folds and taste her fully. Her honey coats my tongue, and I'm pleased to find I can still lengthen the slick muscle. I burrow it deep inside her tight cunt and groan as she fucks my face.

Curling my thrusting muscle deep, Nory erupts with a scream and soaks me with her come. I lick her clean before prowling back up her body. She lifts her hips, seeking my hard cock. Gripping the leaking hardness in my hand, I fit it to her entrance and fill her in one thrust.

I capture her moan in my mouth as I rock into her body again and again.

"Eryx," she moans. "Please."

Turning her head, she bares her throat to me in a silent plea. I kiss her cheeks and lick over the scar of my initial bites. They will be permanent once she is changed—my mark upon her forever. I shiver in delight.

"I love you, Nory," I growl against her throat.

"I love you." Her eyes fly open, and her pussy clenches on me. "Bite me."

I do as she bids me, like the loyal servant I am. I break through her soft flesh, and her blood is as decadent as ever. It coats my tongue and flows down my throat. Our hearts pound together, and the threads of souls weave tight.

Nory lets out a cry and scores my back as she comes. I drink her down as I take my own pleasure. Spilling my seed deep within her, I'm awash in pleasure unlike ever before. Once I've given her all my seed and I feel her body relax, I pull out of her and lick up her wound.

Nuzzling her close, I pull her shivering body into my arms. Kissing her lips, I savor our mingling tastes.

"How long will it take?" she asks, voice already beginning to slur from exhaustion.

"I don't know."

Honestly, I don't. We are in uncharted territory. Whatever the future holds, we will blaze the path together. Of that I am certain. I look down at her and everything clicks into place. Had I never come to this forsaken town, our paths would've never crossed, and I would've been undone. This cruel world would've crushed her, as it does so many with kind hearts.

Instead, we've found each other forever. In this moment, I am more grateful to my maker than I ever have been before. If I had not been different, I wouldn't have this. Every lonely moment—every starving hour—led me to Nory. Both our journeys were challenging, but we found each other.

That is all that matters.

"Will you hold me until it's over?"

A yawn sneaks up on her. Kissing her forehead, I draw her deeper into my chest.

"Always," I say. "Forever."

EPILOGUE

ERYX - TEN YEARS LATER

We shouldn't remain in this town for much longer. Rumors are already spreading amongst the villagers here. Whispers of a strange plague or merciless killer are on the lips of noble lords and drunkards alike. They all repeat the same stories. Innocent men being snatched off the street—drained of their blood and their corpses left to rot in dark alleyways. Each morning, new bodies are discovered, leading the townspeople to wonder just what curse has befallen their land.

They are wrong on two accounts.

Firstly, this land is not cursed—we will leave it in peace once our hunger has been sated. Secondly—and most importantly—those men were not innocent. My wife saw to that. They were evil men with rotten souls, just like the one she is entreating with now.

The man leans against the wall of the tavern, ignorant of the danger prowling in his shadow and standing right before him. His dark hair shines in the low light, and the crinkles around his brown eyes deepen as he grins at Nory. Her smile is compelling, but I note its brittleness. After all, no one brings her more genuine smiles than I.

After a decade together, I know my wife better than myself. Still, whenever I watch her interact with these men, I can't help but grind my teeth together, counting down the seconds until we can drain them together. This man needs killing more than most—an adulterer who leaves his wife and child to fend for themselves while he wastes all their coin inside gambling halls.

He is far from the only man of his ilk polluting this town. It's why we've lingered here for so long. Once I turned Nory, we had struck another bargain, one that included our desire to see the world together and only claim the lives of those who deserved it.

And of course, to love each other completely and endlessly until this world becomes dust.

All three were easy enough to agree to. I had Nory; everything else was just details. If it weren't for our need to feed, I'd swear we would never pull ourselves apart. As it was, this hunting trip has been more than successful, and we'll be satisfied for a while. Long enough to travel further up the coastline and reach the northern beaches.

Just the thought of taking Nory in the sand—her beautiful body glowing in the moonlight as I pound into her until she screams is making me impatient for this final hunt to be over.

I watch her manipulate the man, smiling and nodding—I don't have to read his mind to know he's thanking his good fortune for putting her on his path. Indeed, the skills she honed back in the Snowlands have become instrumental.

After she had awoken from the change, we made our way back to her cottage that the townsfolk had decimated. Most of the beams holding up the missing roof were still smoldering as we made our way through. The place had been thoroughly ransacked before being set ablaze. Nory—clever woman that she is—had hidden away her earnings under a floorboard in the kitchen.

Taking what she could manage from the house, she had lingered in the doorway. I hadn't said anything as she said goodbye to her mother's house. I only offered her the solace of my body, which she accepted greedily. After that, we made our way to her mother's grave, where she set down a fresh bouquet and said goodbye to her one final time, stating she would never come back. Whispering to the headstone, she had found her happiness. She had risen from the grave, and the determination in her gaze burned me alive.

That night, her first kills were the men who had torched her house. It had been a thrill to watch her hunt. She was decisive and cutthroat—wild and unabandoned. The sight of her covered in their blood with eyes like two green flames was more than I could bear. We fucked right beside their corpses, her moans echoing around us in the night as she begged me for more.

Nory has a healthy bloodlust, but just like me, our hunger for each other supersedes everything else.

Looking at her now under the orange glow of the torches illuminating the side of the tavern, it's hard to believe my good fortune. That, against all the odds, Nory is mine. My maker gave me a way to have her forever, and I'll never stop being grateful for it—for her.

The man before us is a fool—they all are. As a human, she had been a temptation, one that none of them could deny. Now, her beauty is striking—deadly. Her pale skin is smooth and supple, dusted with golden freckles. Her movements are all predatory grace. If he had been paying attention to her in the tavern and not absorbed with thoughts about how he was going to bed her, he would've noticed her not touch the food or wine on the table before her.

Even now, he should notice the sheen to her green eyes— the primal edge.

Just like all the others, he discerns nothing. A grateful lamb to the slaughter, ignoring the danger in front of him because he's too preoccupied with her beauty. He won't be the first to succumb to this fate and surely will not be the last.

Nory's eyes flash as she looks in my direction before nodding and peeling off the wall. Her white fur-trimmed cloak drags behind her down the dark alley. The man follows on her heels. She glances back, smiling at him, but her eyes find mine. One sinful wink is all I need to push off the wall I'm hiding behind and stalk after them.

I can sense his movements before he makes them. With my silent steps, the man never realizes I'm there waiting—waiting for him to lift his hand and reach for her. His outstretched hand barely grazes the fur atop her shoulders when I strike. My hand encases his throat as I slam his body against the brick wall.

Blood blooms on the wall behind his head, and a choked moan rattles from his lungs. He can't scream—not when I have his crushed windpipe in my palm. I lean into his face, letting madness kindle in my gaze. Even in his pain-ridden, delirious state, he still manages to turn white. Snarling into his face, I condemn him to death.

"Did you think you could touch her? *My wife*," I spit.

He gargles a denial, kicking his feet in an attempt at freedom.

"It will be the last mistake you ever make."

Nory giggles softly at my side, her hand trailing up my back.

"So possessive," she sighs. "Let's feast, my love. This one is beginning to annoy me."

Without another word, we take our spots on either side of him. The man attempts to scream, but only a harsh whistle leaks from his throat. In unison, we sink our teeth into his neck and silence him forever. Together we drink his sticky, warm blood until there is none left. Pulling back, we let his corpse clatter to the ground.

I turn towards Nory, taking her in my arms. My mouth swoops down to capture her lips, licking a scarlet drop from the corner of her mouth. She grins up at me, eyes shining like emeralds.

"Wonderful as always, Nory. You've become quite the actress," I compliment.

Nory hums low in her throat, and my cock hardens at the red flush of her cheeks. I've had her in every depraved way imaginable, and yet she still manages to blush. I kiss her flush as she takes my hand, leading me away from the corpse in the alley.

We break onto the main strip of road. With the news of our kills spreading, the streets have become more barren. Even so, with my new form, I can travel more easily. There's no mistaking me for a human man, but under the cover of darkness and a well-placed hood, I can blend in, especially when I'm with Nory. No one glances in my direction with her perfection at my side.

Fluffy snowflakes fall from the dark sky above. They collect along her brow and in her red hair. Nory tips her face up towards them, the cold turning the tip of her nose red. Her warm skin slides against my palm as we make our way towards the end of the main street.

"I've grown bored of this town," she announces. "We should go somewhere warm next.

I chuckle.

"Wherever you want. I was thinking the beaches up north could be nice."

"So agreeable. You are the perfect husband—I am the envy of all females."

My hand tightens on her as I share her smile. While her

tone is teasing, her eyes are serious and filled with love. We married the night after her transition, not by any priest or councilman, but as two beings deep in *The Woods* confessing their love and binding their souls together. It was a stronger vow than any human one could offer us.

We were one—entwined forever. Who needs rings when I have her soul woven with mine?

Nory's steps slow at my side. She turns on the gravel that's quickly being covered by snow. I look to see what's captured her attention. Before us is a dilapidated structure. An old oak door hangs off rusted hinges. The shutters on the windows are missing. Countless holes decorate the roof, and the spire atop is cracked and leaning to one side. The front steps are rotten.

If I'm not mistaken, this looks to be a—

"Come on," Nory nudges, dragging me by the hand.

I catch the wicked glint in her eye. The scent of her arousal engulfs me with its heady sweetness. My cock rises in anticipation.

"Naughty," I say, feet creaking along the wooden porch.

"I have no idea what you're talking about."

Nory giggles as she rips open the old door. The darkness inside envelopes us as she pulls me in after her. Turning in my arms, she grips the front of my cloak and pushes up on her toes to capture my mouth. She tastes like honey and smells of fresh roses. My hands roam over her back as our tongues dance together. My wife surrenders to my kiss as she always does.

"Do you need my cock?" I ask against her ear.

Nory's moan catches in her throat. I can see her legs rubbing together underneath her dress. Her sweet pussy calls to me—begging for the relief only I can give it.

"Always," she sighs. "Hunting makes me crave you more than normal."

The room around us is bare save for a few unlit pillar candles and overturned pews. A small table is off to the side, covered in dust. With a wave of my hand, I clean it and settle Nory atop it. Her hands fall to my shoulders, trying to remove my cloak. Gripping the hem of her dress, I push it up, revealing her lithe, stocking-covered thighs.

"Yes," she hisses. "Please, Eryx."

Her pussy is bare to my gaze. Moisture coats her inner thighs, and my mouth waters. Her face is contorted in pleasure, and I've barely touched her yet. One lick of my tongue will set her off. Usually, I want to offer her a quick release, but tonight, I want to toy with my wife a bit. Leaning down, I capture her mouth, feeling her thighs wrap around my hips.

My cock pushes at the front of my pants, eagerly meeting her wet heat. She drags herself along my hardness, moaning into my mouth. I kiss down her jaw, licking a path along her throat before stopping at the neckline of her dress. I taste the smooth skin of her breasts and lick her hard nipples through the fabric of her gown.

Nory's head falls back as I kiss her lower. The intoxicating scent of her overwhelms me. Dragging my face over my stomach, my hands wrap around her knees. Lowering myself to the floor, I—

A scream rips through the room. Nory's whole body tenses and thrashes against mine. Protective instincts surge within me, and I cover her body in an instant. Glancing around us, I try to look for any sign of danger. There is nothing—only dusty books and shattered stained glass.

"What—what is that thing?" Nory whispers, pointing towards the front of the room.

I glance in the direction and stop short. How had I not noticed it before? The broken and overturned pews form a haphazard aisle that leads to an altar. Atop it are a few moth-bitten chairs, an old leather-bound book, and a massive gargoyle.

This one has been frozen for some time. Cobwebs form

between its massive set of wings, splayed behind it in attack. Even in its crouched position, the figure is enormous. Clawed hands rest between its massive thighs, and its face is pulled into a snarl. Rows of razor-sharp teeth glint back. The pale marble it's hewn from glows in the dim light. The figure is imposing and unsettling.

"A gargoyle," I say, helping Nory off the table.

She smooths down her dress and walks towards it. Staring up at the large creature, her brows furrow. Reaching out a hand towards it, she quickly snatches it back. An ancient magic pulses from the being, and I have no doubt she can sense it. Looking over her shoulder at me, she raises a quizzical brow.

"They were made to protect churches—ordained as protectors by the Order of the True Faith. Centuries ago, something happened. They broke with the Order and became trapped in these stone prisons." I shrug. "No one knows what caused the change."

"Aren't they supposed to keep guard on the roof?"

"Maybe this one got lost."

Wrapping my arms around her, I pull her back flush against my front. My hands roam all over her while my lips devour her neck and shoulders. Nory sighs and leans her head to the side. Slipping my hand into the front of her gown, I palm her breast and gently worry her nipple.

Her gasp is music to my ears.

"Good girl. Now, let's get back to—"

"It just blinked at me."

I chuckle against her skin, my hand dragging along her hip.

"It's just your imagination."

Nory whirls in my grasp, breaking free of my hold. Her green eyes are unamused.

"We are not fucking while that thing watches," she hisses, jerking her thumb at the gargoyle. "Besides, fornicating in a church? Doesn't that seem a little—"

"Blasphemous?" I offer.

Her cheeks pink as she nods.

"You won't let me take you in an abandoned church, but a graveyard was fine? Fickle thing you are."

Nory's lips flatten into a line.

"Or I won't let you fuck me at all," she grumbles.

My laugh echoes around us as I take her into my arms and pull her away from the altar.

"Idle threats, Nory," I murmur into her hair. "But we'll do this your way."

Once we are outside, the snow is coming down in earnest. It collects on our shoulders. Nory shivers against me. Hefting her into my arms, she squeals as her legs leave the ground. I cradle her against me as I walk quickly towards the old farming cottage we've been staying in.

The man who lived here was our first victim—his wife and young son fled upon finding his body. It seemed a shame to let such a cozy home go to waste. Kicking open the old door, I latch the iron lock and set Nory on her feet. With a wave of her hand, the hearth ignites, and orange flames lick over both of us.

Together we work to shed our wet clothes and shoes. Once we are done, our bare skin meets. My cock pushes between us, already leaking moisture. Nory bites her lip and stares up at me. Capturing her around the waist, she giggles as I deposit her on the bed—her long hair fans out behind her for only a moment. Nory's predatory grace is on full display as she rolls onto her stomach and then pushes up onto all fours.

Looking over her shoulder at me, she curves her spine, presenting each of her little pink holes to me.

"I can never resist you, husband," she sighs, tilting her hips towards me. "You know what I want."

Kneeling behind her, the bed creaks at my weight. Cotton sheets cushion my knees as I grip the globes of her ass and lick her back entrance. Nory moans, her hands gripping the simple headboard. Her back bows as I lick again, jiggling my tongue into her tight hole. Moisture glides out of her pussy in a stream. My mouth waters, needing to collect it all.

"Eryx," she purrs. "Please."

"Again? I already had your ass this morning."

Her verdant eyes flash.

"Are you going to tell me no?" she pouts, lips twisting into a frown.

Rising behind her, I take my hard cock in my hand. Gliding it through her slit, I use her wetness to coat the head. I spit down onto her back entrance and gently use my thumb to press into her. Nory's moans are the sweetest sound. The scent of our coupling fills the small cottage.

My ridges drag along her greedy clit. Sweat breaks out along her back. A flush appears on her pale skin as she rubs herself against me. Her whole body shakes in anticipation of my possession.

"Please, Eryx. I need you, husband," she begs. "Fuck me. Don't make me wait."

"Greedy," I snarl, but do as she bids me.

I fit my cock to her ass. The pink hole stretches around my length. It's used to my invasion, but it is as tight as the first time I fucked her here. Nory cries out as I surge all the way inside her. She takes every inch of me, even as I flatten her to the bed —the mounds of her ass press against my hips as I'm fully sheathed inside her.

I could come from this alone—just being inside her.

"I'm not going to last," I growl between clenched teeth. "Be a good girl and come quickly."

Propping her hips up, I withdraw and plunge deep again. Her cries are harsh. The brutality of my taking is what she desires above all else. Nory gives me the picture of true supplication. I reward her surrender with the sneaking of my hand to the apex of her thighs to play with her clit.

Nory claws at the sheets, shredding them in her fists.

She is all I need now and forever. We are one—each other's only family. The thought of getting her pregnant hadn't been a concern when we were first together. I was a death omen—my seed was as dead as my heart. Now things are different. We had discussed starting a family. I will admit that the image of Nory, swollen with my child, is a beautiful fantasy. However, we cannot deny our greed for each other.

We decided that for now, she will take the contraceptive herbs and we will be it for each other. I wouldn't have it any other way. We have an eternity to change our minds—for now, all I need is Nory. She is more than enough.

Overwhelmed by lust for my wife, I listen to her keening moans and know she's close. Her ass clenches around my thrusting cock. Her whole body trembles, and when I graze her clit again, she erupts with a scream of my name. I follow her into pleasure, spraying torrents of hot seed into her tight ass.

I come down atop her shaking body and lick sweat from her shoulders. Nory gasps into the sheets. Once we have caught our breath, I roll us onto our sides and spoon my body around her. My hand traces along her lovely face, taking note of each freckle—all forty-seven of them.

"I love you, Nory."

She grins.

"You better."

Chuckling, I nuzzle into her side and feel her yawn. Exhaustion covers us like a blanket. I will need her again soon —or she will reach for me in the middle of slumber and ride me with her glorious breasts bouncing. I welcome it all. Nory is my heart, my soul, my love. We will never be parted.

Those lonely centuries feel so far away in these moments. I can hardly remember the male I was before Nory. He was nothing but a husk of hunger and sadness. Now, there is only warmth and happiness. Each day with Nory is a precious gift. One I won't stop protecting.

No matter what the future holds, one thing is certain. We will face it together, no matter what. Each day, I'll show Nory just how much I love her. Over and over again.

Endlessly.

DON'T MISS THE NEXT ONE!

A fallen sister looking for salvation and a monster looking for redemption. One night of passion will change everything! Coming January 2026.

Holiday-themed monster romances for those who want a little extra spice on Kindle Unlimited!

ACKNOWLEDGMENTS

I want to thank all of you for picking up *A Kiss From a Revenant*! I hope you all enjoyed this spooky/gothic monster romance. I'll definitely have to write more macabre romances soon!

I'd like to thank my beta/ARC teams, my patrons, and all of you who've shared or continue to support my work. See you in the next one!

xoxo Charlotte

ABOUT THE AUTHOR

Charlotte Swan is twenty-seven year old, living in Chicago. When she is not dreaming about being whisked away to a world filled with magic and sexy monsters, she is busy being a freelance social media marketer and full-time smut lover. To read her debut novel *Taken by the Dark Elf King*, hear about her upcoming projects, or to connect with her on social media please find her on her website or by scanning the code below.

www.authorcharlotteswan.com

www.ingramcontent.com/pod-product-compliance
Lightning Source LLC
Chambersburg PA
CBHW031542310726
48971CB00008B/2591